"I've been wondering what the most beautiful woman in the room is doing hiding in a corner."

The wholly masculine voice sent a shiver down Emily's spine.

He was dressed in a tux, and the black suit was the perfect complement to Javier's dark hair and eyes while the crisp white shirt contrasted with his gorgeously tanned skin. He'd brushed his hair back for the ceremony, but a hint of natural wave threatened to break free from the staid style with only the slightest provocation.

Like a woman running her fingers through the dark strands…

Curling her fingernails into her palms, Emily forced her gaze back to the ballroom. But even with her eyes locked on the dance floor, she heard the rustle of palms as Javy stepped closer. Felt him against skin left bare by the strapless gown.

Dear Reader,

Imagine a dream wedding, planned to perfection in every detail…except one. The bride is no longer the one getting married. That's the situation Emily Wilson finds herself in after calling off her engagement days before the wedding. She has little choice but to pick up the pieces and move on…with a little help from the sexy best man, Javier Delgado.

I think we've all had dreams that didn't come true in the way we expected, and yet in the end, have flourished in ways we never imagined. Or perhaps they've come true after we've nearly given up on them.

I hope you enjoy *The Wedding She Always Wanted* and Emily's journey to realizing the only part of a perfect wedding she needs is the perfect groom.

Stacy Connelly

THE WEDDING SHE ALWAYS WANTED

STACY CONNELLY

SPECIAL EDITION

Published by Silhouette Books

America's Publisher of Contemporary Romance

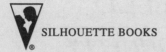 SILHOUETTE BOOKS

Recycling programs
for this product may
not exist in your area.

ISBN-13: 978-0-373-65515-1

THE WEDDING SHE ALWAYS WANTED

Copyright © 2010 by Stacy Cornell

Visit Silhouette Books at www.eHarlequin.com

Printed in U.S.A.

Books by Stacy Connelly

Silhouette Special Edition

All She Wants for Christmas #1944
Once Upon a Wedding #1992
The Wedding She Always Wanted #2033

STACY CONNELLY

has dreamed of publishing books since she was a kid, writing stories about a girl and her horse. Eventually, boys made it onto the page as she discovered a love of romance and the promise of happily ever after.

When she is not lost in the land of make-believe, Stacy lives in Arizona with her two spoiled dogs. She loves to hear from readers and can be contacted at stacyconnelly@cox.net or www.stacyconnelly.com.

Thanks to all my friends who understand
when a glazed look comes over my eyes,
I'm not ignoring them…I'm brainstorming!

Chapter One

Emily Wilson had spent years practicing her smile. Not too wide, or her eyes would squint. Not too small, or the expression looked fake. Somewhere in between was the perfect smile Emily modeled, even when smiling was the last thing she wanted to do.

Despite the years of practice, she couldn't remember when she'd had a harder time holding on to that smile. But then again, she'd never had to survive a day like today. Her wedding day.

Only she wasn't the one getting married.

The ballroom looked exactly as she'd imagined. White cloaked tables circled the black granite dance floor. Pink roses and silver candles floated in glass bowls, the light reflected by mirrored chargers beneath. In every corner, towering plants reached right up to a moonlit night revealed by the soaring glass ceiling. A romantic ballad played as the bride and groom met for their first dance, love shining in their eyes.

Just like she imagined, Emily thought, her stomach twisting, except for the identity of the bride and groom.

"How are you holding up?" a quiet voice asked behind her.

Emily turned to face her older sister. Wearing a pink bridesmaid's dress identical to her own, Aileen's brows were pulled together in a concerned frown. "I'm fine," Emily answered automatically. "The wedding was beautiful, and no one deserves it more than Kelsey."

As little as a week ago Emily could never have imagined that the wedding her cousin had planned would end up as Kelsey's own wedding to Connor McClane, Emily's high school boyfriend.

"And how many times have you said that line today?"

"To everyone who's actually had the courage to come up to me. Which, considering the number of people here, hasn't been all that many. Everyone is much too busy talking *about* me to actually bother talking *to* me."

"Well, it's not every day that a wedding goes off as planned, only with a completely different bride and groom," Aileen noted.

"And it's not every day a woman learns her fiancé got another girl pregnant and proposed only to get back into his family's good graces."

It had, in fact, been Thursday, mere days before her wedding.

Shoving hurt and humiliation aside, Emily insisted, "Besides, it's not just a line. I am happy for Kelsey. And for Connor."

Connor had come back to town with the specific purpose of stopping Emily's wedding to Todd Dunworthy. He was the one to discover Todd's hidden agenda. Along the way, Connor had also fallen in love with Kelsey.

"I know you are," Aileen said, "and we're all glad Connor found out what Todd was up to before you married the jerk. I still can't believe how completely he fooled all of us."

But Todd *had* fooled all of them, including Emily's parents, who had seen him as the perfect future son-in-law. Maybe she should have felt better, knowing she wasn't the only idiot in the bunch, but she didn't. Instead, the betrayal had shaken her foundations.

Her whole life she'd followed the plan her parents had laid out for her—going to the right schools, wearing the right clothes, being seen with the right people. She'd always done what she was told, never crossed the line…except for a brief moment of teenaged rebellion, when she jumped over it and into Connor's arms.

Intense, rough around the edges, Connor McClane had been nothing like the boys at her prep school. For a few short weeks, she'd been thrilled by the youthful infatuation and by veering so far off course from the map her parents had drawn out for her life. But before long she'd realized dating Connor wasn't as much about following her own dreams as it was about defying her parents. Knowing Connor deserved better, she'd broken things off with him.

Almost ten years later his call to congratulate her on her engagement had come as a surprise, and she'd impulsively sent him a wedding invitation. A decision that had changed all of their lives, she thought as she watched Connor spin his new bride into his arms.

"Connor saw through Todd right from the start," Emily said.

So why hadn't she?

Was she that gullible, that naive? How could she trust her own feelings—or trust in love—again?

"Connor's a P.I. He's trained to look for those kinds of things. Don't be so hard on yourself," Aileen advised. After a few more minutes she said, "I'm going to go up and say good-night to Ginny and Duncan. I promised I'd tuck them in."

Aileen's daughter and son had been the flower girl and ring bearer. Like Emily, Aileen and her family were staying the night at the hotel.

"Give them a kiss for me."

"I will." Aileen disappeared around the tall palms sheltering Emily from the rest of the room.

Maybe she should go with her sister, Emily thought. Not that Aileen needed help with her kids, but any escape was a good escape.

She'd almost decided on the cowardly action when a deep voice murmured, "I've been wondering what the most beautiful woman in the room is doing hiding in a corner."

The wholly masculine sound sent a shiver down Emily's spine. She knew without turning who stood behind her. She was a little surprised she hadn't felt electricity arcing along her nerve endings, like an early warning system, before Javier Delgado ever spoke.

From the moment they first met at Kelsey and Connor's impromptu engagement party, Javy had had an undeniable effect on her. But Connor's best friend and best man also had a reputation as a ladies' man. And right now, after what had happened with Todd, he was exactly the kind of man she wanted to stay far, far away from.

Unfortunately, being in the wedding party together meant their paths had crossed more often than she would have liked in the last few days. And darn it if her pulse hadn't skipped a beat every single time.

Turning to face him, she offered a small smile, keeping her expression as remote as possible, a smooth surface completely hiding the turmoil beneath—or so she hoped. "Javy," she said with a chiding tone, "don't you know the bride is the most beautiful woman in the room?"

Javier grinned, and Emily knew her facade might have

been as smooth as glass, but as transparent, as well. At least where this man was concerned.

Whenever he looked at her, Emily sensed he saw through her—through the perfect smile, through the too-polite chit-chat, through to all the insecurities and failures she sought to hide. While she—she couldn't read him at all.

He was too handsome, too sexy, too much of everything she'd recently learned to distrust.

He was dressed in a tux. The black suit was the perfect complement to his dark hair and eyes, while the crisp white shirt contrasted with his gorgeously tanned skin. He'd brushed his hair back for the ceremony, but a hint of natural wave threatened to break free with only the slightest provocation.

Like a woman running her fingers through the dark strands…

Curling her fingernails into her palms, Emily forced her gaze back to the ballroom. But even with her eyes locked on the dance floor, she heard the rustle of palms as Javy stepped closer. Felt him against skin left bare by the strapless gown.

The aftershave he wore blended with the flowers and vanilla candles, providing a masculine element missing from the too-feminine scents. His breath stirred the fine hair at the nape of her neck, and Emily had the foolish thought that she should have worn her hair down.

Like any hairstyle could possibly provide protection against a man like Javier Delgado.

"Kelsey does look amazing, doesn't she?"

His words barely registered. He hadn't just brushed his lips against her ear when he spoke, had he? No, he wouldn't have. He couldn't have….

Maybe if she asked him to repeat the sentence, he'd do it again, and she'd know for sure.

An unfamiliar heat pooled in her belly, sapping the strength from her legs. The warning system that failed her earlier rang out loud and clear, but Emily couldn't bring herself to step away. She was afraid if she moved at all, it would be to sink into the tall, masculine body surrounding her.

"I…um…" Emily swallowed. "Yes, Kelsey looks beautiful."

She and Aileen had styled her cousin's curly red hair into an elegant twist and applied a sophisticated, smoky-eyed makeup, which down-to-earth Kelsey rarely wore. But Kelsey's gown was too heavenly for anything less. Thanks to her friendship with a local dress designer, Kelsey had had a gorgeous ivory strapless gown altered in a matter of days, and even though the dress wasn't custom-made, the fit certainly was.

But Emily knew it wasn't the hair or the makeup or the wedding gown. The love and happiness glowing in her expression as she gazed at her new husband made Kelsey the most beautiful woman there.

"And I don't think I've ever seen Connor so happy," Javier added.

"You sound surprised." Emily turned to face Javy, thinking she'd be better off if she could keep an eye on him. Or maybe not, she realized as her heart did another tap dance inside her chest when she gazed up at his handsome face.

"I guess I am. My friend never struck me as a 'falling head over heels for a woman' kind of guy."

Emily had a feeling Javy's statement said more about his own relationships than it did about Connor's. "Because the two of you are so alike?"

"Used to be," he said easily enough, but the slight frown pulling at his eyebrows contradicted the unconcerned acceptance. "But things change."

"Yes, they do…." Emily's voice trailed off as three middle-aged women walked by, exchanging knowing looks and smug smiles.

"Hello, Emily," one called out, arching her eyebrows and

making a point of looking from Emily to Javy and back again, their seclusion in the out-of-the-way corner suddenly taking on a salacious air.

Managing a nod, she watched the women walk away, heads bent together as they whispered to one another.

"Who the he—heck are they?"

Face flaming, Emily said, "Those are some of my mother's *friends.*"

But Emily was well aware that friends of her mother often had daughters her own age. Daughters Emily had beaten out in long-ago beauty pageants or for homecoming queen or for the lead role in some forgotten play. They were more than happy to see her publicly humiliated.

Keeping her gaze averted, Emily stared into the distance, not wanting to see the pity in Javy's dark eyes.

"You know," he said softly, "I think you might be one of the bravest women I've ever met."

Emily let out a sharp laugh, the sound grating like broken glass against her throat. "And here I was, just thinking I'm the world's biggest coward."

Tears burned her eyes at the admission. Ducking her head, Emily turned away from Javy, horrified by the thought of breaking down in front of him. She didn't make it more than a few yards when she heard his steps on the granite floor behind her.

Catching her arm, he steered her to the left. "Come on. No more standing on the sidelines. Let's dance."

Vaguely aware of a romantic ballad playing in the background, Emily shook her head. "No. Forget it."

"Why?"

"Because I'm not dancing," she argued as he turned her toward him.

"Why not?"

"I've given people enough reason to talk about me. Last thing I need to do is anything else to attract attention."

Javy smiled slowly. "Too late."

Emily didn't realize what he meant until he slid an arm around her lower back and pulled her body into his. He'd led her to the center of the dance floor, and unless she wanted to walk off mid-dance, she had little choice but to stay where she was. And when her arms automatically wrapped around his broad shoulders, she knew she wouldn't be going anywhere.

His dark eyes looked almost as velvety black as the night sky above, and the sexy spark she saw in his gaze put the Milky Way to shame. He danced like a man who knew how to move his body…and how to make a woman respond. His hands trailed down her spine to the curve of her hips; his thighs brushed against hers in time with the music, each step making her breath catch in anticipation of the next. With the stiff stays lining the strapless bodice of her dress, she couldn't possibly feel the beat of his heart. Which meant the wild, crazy rhythm was hers alone…

"Relax," Javy commanded, his voice a husky whisper in her ear. "Forget that anyone's watching."

Emily *had* forgotten about the guests lining the edges of the dance floor. Any tension he had picked up on was strictly from locking her knees to keep from puddling at his feet. She tried to take a calming breath, only to inhale his cologne, the enticing scent drawing her closer to the spot where his broad shoulder met the tanned column of his neck.

"Unless you want to give them something to really talk about," he murmured, and she doubted he meant the scene she'd make running from the dance floor.

"No. I couldn't," she said, her voice a weak, broken sound.

"Come on. You can't be that worried about what people are going to say."

"I'm here, aren't I? The only thing worse than being here and having all these people talk about me behind my back would be to stay home and have them talk about me without any restraint at all."

"So show 'em you don't care," he encouraged, lifting a hand and running his index finger from the nape of her neck down…over her bare skin…until he hit the top of her dress, where he traced the line of the zipper to the small of her back.

Half surprised the small metal teeth didn't simply melt away, Emily swallowed hard and searched for an argument to keep herself from doing the same. "I *do* care. I *should* care. Today was supposed to be my wedding day. I was supposed to be marrying the man I loved and—"

"But you didn't. And you're relieved."

"Of course I'm relieved. Who would want to be married to someone who cheated and lied?"

"I mean, you're relieved because you *didn't* love him."

Emily pulled back far enough to meet his gaze. If his dark eyes had slowly peeled away her clothes, she wouldn't have been surprised—he had that kind of reputation. But she hadn't anticipated the way his knowing look stripped bare all the insecurities she'd tried to hide. Totally exposed, she struggled to duck behind an indignant front.

"What makes you so sure? You don't know me. You don't know—"

"I know when a woman's in love, and I know when she's heartbroken. And you, sweetheart, are neither."

Javy let Emily go at the end of the dance. He couldn't help watching her walk away. The gown she wore fit her willowy curves to perfection, drawing his eyes to her slender waist and the flare of her hips. The color—a soft, innocent pink—made her skin look even creamier. She had a grace and bearing that spoke of her wealth and pedigree. He would have gladly danced with her all night—breathing in the scent of peaches on her skin, following the fragrance from the curve of her neck, left bare by her upswept hair, to the hollow of her throat, to the valley between her breasts—but the worry clouding her blue eyes had told him how truly concerned she was by what the high-society guests around them thought.

Too bad she hadn't taken him up on his offer to give the crowd something to talk about. His blood heated at the thought of Emily kissing him in front of the whole crowd, of discovering her unique taste, feeling the slow, soft slide of her lips against his own… But he supposed it would require something bigger than dumping a fiancé she didn't really love to shake up her world that much.

Making his way to the bar, he ordered a beer. Champagne toasts were likely the thing, but he had simpler tastes. He'd taken his first sip from the bottle when an exuberant hand clapped down on his shoulder.

"Hey, having fun?"

Javy turned to meet Connor's grin. "You bet. This is my kind of party," he said wryly. "Loved the ice sculpture, by the way. What the hell was it supposed to be? Some kind of snake?"

"A swan," his friend said, only to admit a split second later, "I think. Anyway, this is what Kelsey wanted. Her dream wedding." As he spoke, his gaze immediately sought out his new wife, who was dancing with her uncle.

Javy figured he could have dumped the melting serpent/swan into his friend's lap and he wouldn't have noticed. "I'm happy for you, man. Really." He winced, hearing the doubt he was trying a little too hard to hide.

"Yeah, right." Connor slanted Javy a glance that reminded him how well they knew each other.

"Sorry. I mean, don't get me wrong. Kelsey's a great girl, but—"

"You didn't think I'd ever settle down," Connor said, filling in the details. His gaze met Kelsey's from across the ballroom, and he smiled. "Things change."

He'd said the same to Emily. "Yeah, guess so."

"Except for you." Turning back to Javy, Connor said, "Look, I know you're still all about playing the field, but you gotta know Emily's not up for the game."

Javy pulled back in surprise. "Hell, Connor, you haven't warned me away from a girl since we were both interested in Alicia Martin in the fifth grade. Are you sure you married the right woman? Emily's—"

"Emily is Kelsey's cousin," Connor interrupted, leaning forward enough to warn Javy not to finish his thought. "I'm just looking out for her. She's family now. You understand."

"Yeah, sure," Javy agreed as Kelsey waved her husband over to the dance floor.

He understood because at one time Connor had considered *Javy* family. They'd practically grown up together, covering each other's backs and pulling each other through some rough times.

"Things change," he mumbled, lifting the beer bottle to his lips for another drink.

Connor wasn't the first of his friends to get married and likely wouldn't be the last. But Javy had no intention of following that line down the aisle. Not now, not ever.

Connor was right about Javy liking to play the field. It had been years since he'd had trouble forgetting a woman, and ever since then, they had come and gone, none of them sticking around long enough to etch a place in his life or in his heart. He had no reason to believe Emily would be any different.

Now that the wedding was over, there'd be little chance

of their paths crossing again and less reason for her to cross his thoughts.

No, he definitely wouldn't have any problem forgetting Emily Wilson, he thought as an exotic brunette at the end of the bar caught his eye. Her ruby-red lips curved in invitation, and he waited for the familiar kick of interest to flare. He could send over a drink—a cosmopolitan, he figured—strike up a conversation and be well on his way to forgetting. He'd learned, thanks to his friends' weddings, that a reception was the perfect place to first meet a woman. After all, half the work was done for him. The candles, the flowers, the romantic music were already in place. It was easy. Maybe too easy…

When the bartender came by, Javy didn't order a cosmo or any other kind of break-the-ice drink. Instead, he handed over a few bills for his beer and turned to watch Emily in the out-of-the-way corner where he'd first spotted her.

He wondered if she knew how completely false her smile looked even from across the room. It didn't come close to reaching her eyes—those beautiful blue eyes with darker flecks, which reminded him of the turquoise gemstones his mother loved.

Emily Wilson was a gorgeous woman, no doubt about it, but if she really smiled—hell, if she laughed—he didn't think a man in the room could resist. Including him.

Good thing it didn't look like she'd be laughing anytime soon.

Twenty minutes, Emily vowed silently. She'd give Connor and Kelsey another twenty minutes to cut the cake, and then she was leaving.

She'd accomplished what she had set out to do by coming to the wedding. First, of course, to see her cousin and Connor get married. And second, to face friends and acquaintances for the first time since calling off the wedding. She'd known the whispers and speculation would only be harder to withstand the more time that passed. So, although she wished she were brave enough to stay until the end—heck, she longed for the courage to stand among the single women and do her darnedest to catch the bouquet—in twenty minutes she was going to live up to her own words and sneak out a side door.

Until then, well, Emily decided she had to go to the restroom. She'd check her makeup, her hair, her dress, her shoes, even her nail polish, and hopefully by the time she completed the head-to-toe inspection, at least a quarter of an hour would have passed.

As she stepped into the gold and marble restroom, the door closed behind her, muffling the sounds of music and laughter coming from the reception. Emily leaned against the door for a second and took her first deep breath in hours. The evening was almost over, and she had survived, proving once and for all that embarrassment could not kill.

Walking over to the vanity and the gilded mirror lit by matching sconces, Emily tried to focus on her hair, to double-check that none of the intricate curls were escaping the upswept style. But she froze, staring into her own reflection. Not checking her eyeliner for smudges or pulling her lip gloss from her beaded purse to dab on a second soft pink coat, but instead taking a good, long look at herself.

What was it about her that she couldn't even inspire faithfulness during a *very* brief engagement? Todd hadn't even waited until the wedding to break his vows. That slap of reality made a dream of lasting love and commitment seem just that—an impossible dream.

Except she had every faith that Connor's love for Kelsey would last. Her cousin had found true love, as had her sister. Her parents' thirty-plus years of marriage proved their lasting commitment. Which meant the dream was only impossible for her…because of something lacking *in* her.

Emily turned the faucets on full blast and roughly scrubbed at her hands. Todd was the one at fault, and she needed to stop blaming herself. Yet the doubts picked away at her self-confidence like hungry, spiteful ravens.

I know when a woman's in love, and I know when she's heartbroken. And you, sweetheart, are neither.

On the dance floor Emily had done her best to dismiss Javy's words. He knew nothing about her. How could he presume to look inside her heart? But the more she had to work to summon up her anger, the more she worried he was right.

She'd been so sure she loved Todd; why else would she have agreed to marry him? And yet hadn't she sensed their relationship wasn't all it should have been? That he spent more time telling her what he thought she wanted to hear than actually talking to her? That they never looked beyond the surface of an engagement that looked good on paper?

She now knew why Todd had been so willing to accept so little. The bitter question was, why had she?

Keeping her gaze away from the mirror, Emily finished washing her hands. She'd just thrown the paper towels away when she heard a burst of laughter coming from the outside hall.

Averse to coming face-to-face with anyone at the moment, Emily grabbed her small purse and ducked into the far stall.

The restroom door opened, letting in a burst of music and laughter, along with two women. "Tell me! I have been dying to hear the whole story."

Emily's stomach immediately clenched at the expectation in the woman's voice.

"Well…" Drawing out the moment, the second woman paused. "From what I heard, she found out her fiancé was cheating on her with the family chef."

"No!"

"Yes, and it gets even worse! It turns out they have a child together. A boy, I think."

"Oh, that is horrible!" the second woman exclaimed, sounding all too overjoyed by the scandal.

Humiliation burned in Emily's cheeks at the delight the women were taking in her embarrassment. The details were wrong but close enough for her to realize her family had once again trusted the wrong person. She hadn't spoken to anyone else about Todd's infidelity or his reasons for proposing. And yet someone—her mother or sister, most likely—had talked to a close friend, no doubt swearing them to secrecy, for all the good it had done.

The betrayal was minor compared to Todd's lying and cheating, but for Emily, it was the last straw.

With a definitive flick of her wrist, she unlocked the stall door. The two women spun in guilty tandem, but Emily didn't spare them a glance. Instead, she moved toward the mirror. She tucked a loose strand of hair behind one ear, keeping her focus on her own reflection as she spoke. "It was the maid, not the chef. And she's still pregnant. The baby hasn't been born yet. If you're going to talk about me, you might as well get the details straight."

A stunned silence accompanied her exit from the restroom— probably the first time either woman had stopped talking since they'd arrived—but Emily didn't feel better. She hadn't thought it possible, but if anything, she actually felt worse.

She was leaving. Now. Before she gave everyone even more to talk about by foolishly bursting into tears at her cousin's reception.

Rounding a corner, she gasped when a pair of strong hands clamped on her shoulders, stopping her from running head-long into a tuxedoed chest. "Whoa! Where's the fire?" Javy's laughter trailed away, and he ducked his head to look into her face. His thick eyebrows lowered over his eyes. "Emily? Are you all right?"

Desperate to escape, she said, "I—I have to get out of here."

"Okay." Without questioning, he draped an arm around her shoulders and guided her toward an exit. But instead of a quick farewell before he went straight back to the reception, he followed her into the summer night air.

Moonlight glinted on the surface of the nearby pool, and the multicolored lights played over the stream pouring from a rock waterfall. The peaceful setting was a sharp contrast to the turmoil churning inside her, reminding Emily this was her problem.

Everyone else was having a good time. Everyone else *should* be having a good time…including Javy. She hadn't missed the hungry looks several women at the reception had slanted in his direction. He could be with any one of them right now.

Ignoring the twinge of regret, she turned to him and said, "You need to go back inside. You're the best man. You have to give the toast and—"

"Already did."

"You did?"

"Yep. Short and sweet, just the way the guests like it. No one came here tonight to hear me talk."

"I'm sorry I missed it." Despite his protest, Emily definitely enjoyed hearing Javy talk. The deep murmur of his voice held a hint of his Hispanic heritage and a trace of good humor, like he was ready to laugh at any given moment.

"Hmm, me, too. I have to say, I was a hit. Especially the love song I recited in Spanish."

Uncertain if she could take him seriously, she protested, "You did not."

"I did. Spanish *is* one of the romance languages, you know."

Pig Latin would be one of the romance languages as long as

Javy was the one speaking it. She was willing to bet every woman in the ballroom had gone a little weak at the knees listening to him, and maybe it was a good thing she *hadn't* been inside.

The memory of their dance still lingered, not only in her mind, but in every part of her body that had brushed his as they swayed together. She could still feel the softness of his hair on her fingertips, the broad shoulders beneath her hands and the press of his thighs against her own….

Desire still tingled along nerve endings every place they had touched, and the last thing she needed was Javy's Spanish love song as a soundtrack.

Holding out his arm, he said, "Come on."

"Where are we going?"

"For a walk. Unless you'd rather be alone."

Emily knew she should take the easy out he'd given her. Not because she actually wanted to be alone, but because being with a man of Javier Delgado's reputation was not smart.

Or maybe it was, she thought suddenly. After feeling like she'd lived her whole life with blinders on, maybe taking a walk with her eyes wide-open was the smartest thing she could do.

Chapter Two

Javy waited for Emily's answer, anticipation picking up a beat inside him that he hadn't felt for years. He wouldn't blame her if she wanted to be alone, but he hoped she'd say yes. A simple moonlight stroll suddenly meant more than his last several relationships combined.

Stupid, he thought. He was the last guy to suffer from wedding fever, but if he didn't know better...

"Won't Connor notice that you're gone?"

Connor was more likely to notice that *both* he and Emily were gone, but Javy wasn't about to point that out. "I'm sure he'll figure I'm around somewhere. Besides, isn't it time for them to take off for their honeymoon?"

"I suppose so." Emily crossed her slender arms, although she couldn't possibly be cold, even with the slight breeze stirring the summer night air.

Javy swore silently. *Emily* would have been leaving on her

honeymoon tonight. While finding out her fiancé was a liar and a cheat—not to mention a moron, because, come on, what kind of idiot cheated on a woman as beautiful as Emily Wilson?—might have been a relief, it still didn't change the fact that all of Emily's plans had come crashing down around her. Not just plans for a wedding or honeymoon, but her whole future. No wonder she was feeling more than a little lost even if she hadn't loved the guy.

"I'm sorry, Emily. I know how hard this must be for you."

She started walking alongside the meandering pool, silently accepting his offer. "We were going to go on a cruise to the Mexican Riviera. Todd had everything planned. Snorkeling in Cabo, windsurfing in Mazatlán, parasailing in Puerto Vallarta..." Her voice trailed off in a memoriam of broken dreams.

"You like windsurfing?" Javy asked, hearing the doubt in his own voice. He had no problem imaging Emily sunning herself on a sandy beach, easily visualizing her long limbs bared by a less-than-nothing bathing suit, but he couldn't picture her riding the waves on a board.

"I've never been. I'm relatively sure I would have hated it," she said lightly. "Just like I would have hated the cruise. I went on a three-day trip right after I graduated high school. Turns out I get seasick. I spent the entire time feeling nauseous in my cabin." She gave a soft laugh. "If you think about it, Todd really did me a favor. It would have been a miserable honeymoon."

Javy had a feeling the misery would have lasted far beyond the honeymoon. He caught her arm and forced her to face him, with the moon shining down like a single interrogator's light-bulb into her turquoise eyes. "Why, Emily?"

A slender shoulder lifted in an eloquent shrug. "He had everything all planned and—"

"I'm not talking about the honeymoon. I'm talking about everything. The engagement, the wedding. Or was that all planned, too? Was it easier to go along with what everyone else wanted than to stop and think about what would make *you* happy?"

"Of course not. I wouldn't have married Todd—I wouldn't marry *anyone*—just to make my parents happy."

"Then why did you agree to marry him?"

"Because I *loved* him. And don't you tell me that I didn't! You don't know me. You don't know how I feel. And from what little I know of you, you don't know what it's like to be in love. You go from woman to woman with less time than it takes you to swap CDs."

You don't know love. Her words echoed in his thoughts, and Javy's jaw tightened as he thought how wrong she was. He knew how love carved out a man's insides, leaving him as hollow as a grinning jack-o'-lantern. He knew too well—and he'd learned his lesson.

But forcing his muscles to relax, he offered her an easygoing smile. "Feel better?"

Her color still high and her eyes snapping with surprising fire, Emily frowned. "What?"

"Seems like that was something you needed to get out. I was wondering if you felt any better."

"I…no." The light in her eyes died, and righteous indignation faded into a quiet mortification. "No. I don't. I'm so sorry. I don't know what got into me. I never yell at people, and that's the second time tonight."

As far as decibel levels went, Emily had been nowhere near yelling, but her words had certainly been sharp enough to hit their mark. Not that he was about to admit that. "Who else did you yell at?"

"I didn't yell exactly…."

"Let me guess. You spoke in a very stern whisper."

Her lips twitched, hinting at a real smile, which he was

becoming more and more eager to see. "No. But I told two women if they were going to talk about me behind my back, they should at least get the story straight."

"Good for you."

"Is it?" Emily questioned. "Good for me? So far, it's only made me feel even worse."

Her gaze pleaded with him, as if asking him to somehow make her feel better. Her sadness and uncertainty touched something inside Javy, a need that made him want to fix whatever was wrong, a desire to see her smile. But memories of Stephanie clawed at his gut, reminding him of his failure, his broken promises and his reasons for staying away from any woman looking for more than the good time he could offer.

Javy didn't know if Emily figured that out on her own, but she turned away and started walking again. "I knew everyone would be talking about me calling off the wedding. I expected that. What I didn't expect was that everyone would know *why* I called off the wedding. That everyone would know Todd had cheated on me."

She turned and looked at him suddenly, too quickly for him to try to school his expression. "You knew already, too, didn't you?"

With moonlight turning her hair to silver and liming her skin with an ethereal glow, she looked like a mythical fantasy brought to life. Javy wasn't a particularly imaginative man, but had Emily suddenly sprouted gossamer wings, he wouldn't have been that surprised. She was amazing, and her ex was an ass.

"I did. When Connor first came back to town, he told me he thought Todd was bad news," he admitted. When Emily's face immediately fell, he cupped her chin until she met his gaze. Her skin felt like silk against his fingertips, and he had to force himself to pay attention to what he was saying instead of her wide, luminous eyes or the pale pink of her lips. "And, yeah, he told me why you broke it off. But Todd's the one who should feel ashamed, Emily. Not you."

"That's what I keep telling myself."

"Eventually, you'll start to believe it. Hell, that's probably why everyone here is talking about what happened. Because they can't believe Todd would be stupid enough to cheat on you."

A corner of her mouth lifted in a smile, which he longed to taste. "Tell me something. Did Connor send you out here to cheer me up?"

Javy gave a short laugh. After the way his friend had warned him off, the last thing Connor would have done was send Javy out to be alone with Emily. "No. That is definitely not why I came out here."

He saw the doubt in her eyes before she turned away from his touch, and Javy really wished he'd been there to see Connor put Todd Dunworthy in his place. But he knew Emily's former fiancé wasn't entirely to blame. After all, something had pushed her to agree to marry a man Javy didn't believe she loved…despite her insistence to the contrary.

As they walked along the imitation river, with only the sound of the water and the distant reception breaking the silence, Javy said, "You know, I didn't think I'd like you. No offense."

After a blink of surprise, Emily recovered and said, "None taken. I'm still not sure I like you."

"Yeah, you do."

She quickly averted her face, a telltale sign she was blushing, even though it was too dark to see.

Denying the temptation to show her exactly how much she was starting to like him, Javy instead said, "I thought you'd be a typical spoiled, rich girl."

"I am."

"Rich, yeah, but not spoiled."

If anything, Emily had a sweet innocence that made Todd Dunworthy's betrayal even more despicable. And gave Javy even more reason to stay away. He didn't do sweet. He didn't do innocent. It was exactly why Connor had warned him away from Emily. And yet here he was…alone with her in a moonlit garden.

"Emily—"

She grabbed his hand, effectively cutting off whatever he might have said. "Did you hear that?" she asked suddenly.

Figuring she wasn't talking about the pulse pounding in his ears at the feel of her soft skin against his own, he asked, "Hear what?"

"It sounded like… It is! That's Ginny and Duncan!"

"Who?"

"The flower girl and ring bearer, also known as my niece and nephew. Their babysitter took them to their room an hour ago, and my sister went up to tuck them in. I'm sure Aileen thinks they're still there."

Emily led the way around a corner, her heels clicking against the cool decking, and sure enough, a pint-size girl stood at the base of a tree, staring up at the branches. Her golden hair was a wild mop of corkscrew curls, and she was wearing a purple T-shirt and plaid pajama bottoms, but earlier she had looked like a miniature version of Emily. Her hair had been swept up into ringlets crowned with miniature roses, and her dress had been a girlish version of Emily's pink gown. Her smile had grown wider with every petal she tossed along the lace runner. Javy guessed she was around six years old.

She wasn't smiling now, though. With her hands on her hips, she announced, "You're gonna be in big trouble, Duncan!"

Only then did Javy realize Duncan, the ring bearer, was somewhere in the tree above them.

"What do the two of you think you're doing out here?" Emily demanded.

As the little girl spun around, her instant look of guilt quickly turned to indignation. "I told him not to, Aunt Emily. I told him he'd get in trouble, but he said if he climbed to the top of the tree, he could see our house. I told him not to, but he did it, anyway, and now he is stuck and is gonna have to stay in the tree forever!"

"Am not!"

Following the sound of the voice overhead, Javy spotted Duncan. He let out a low whistle when he saw how high the little boy had climbed. The gasp at his side told him the moment Emily spotted her nephew.

"Look at that branch!" Her grip tightened on his hand. "We need to call the fire department."

"It's all right. I'll get him," Javy assured her.

"But—"

"Look, whoever you call, it'll be a while before they arrive. I'm here now. I'll get him down. Trust me," said Javy.

Emily looked back up at the tree. The branch Duncan had climbed out on looked too fragile to hold a kitten. The longer it took to get the little boy down… "All right. But be careful."

"See?" Javy said with a cocky grin. "I knew you liked me."

"I'll like you even more if you get my nephew down in one piece," she retorted, doing her best to stay cool and unaffected and knowing she failed by the gleam in his dark eyes.

And when Javy let go of her hand and shrugged his tuxedo jacket off one broad shoulder, cool and unaffected melted into a puddle of desire. Every bit of moisture evaporated from her mouth, and Emily snapped her jaw shut with an audible clink.

Taking off the fitted jacket made perfect sense; acting as if he were stripping down in the privacy of her bedroom did not.

But while Javy's actions might have been completely circumspect, the promise in his eyes was downright scandalous. As if he knew she'd pictured him in her bedroom, and fully intended to one day be there.

"Hold this for me, will you?" he asked.

Emily set her purse aside on the half wall lining the walkway to take the jacket. It was warm from his body heat and held a hint of aftershave, and Emily forced herself to simply fold the garment over her arm, instead of burying her face into the fabric.

Turning back to the tree, Javy studied the branches as he undid the cuffs of the shirt and rolled the sleeves back to reveal muscular forearms dusted with dark hair.

Emily's stomach did a slow roll. She crossed her arms tightly at her waist, trying to stop any more somersaulting from her internal organs, and hoped the jacket hid the telling action. But when Javy bent down to slip off a shoe, she had to ask, "What are you doing?"

He glanced up at her, his teeth flashing in the dim light as he smiled. Whatever he'd used to hold back his hair lost the battle as a thick lock fell across his forehead. Emily's fingers instinctively burrowed deeper into the wool jacket. "Ever climb a tree in dress shoes? It's a sure trip to the emergency room."

Emily glanced down at her strappy gold heels. She'd spent hours practicing on pencil-thin platforms, insuring she could walk gracefully in even the most fashionable—and uncomfortable—shoes. "I don't think I've ever climbed a tree."

After kicking off the second shoe, Javy straightened. He pushed his hair back only to have it spring forward again. "You're kidding, right? Did you have a deprived childhood, or what?"

It was the first time anyone had ever referred to Emily's life as anything other than privileged. Her friends always commented how lucky Emily was to have everything she'd ever wanted. But she wondered if maybe Javy didn't have it right, after all.

"Believe me, socks are the way to go," he added as he stared up at a branch overhead.

Emily would have sworn it was out of reach, but he took a few steps back, enough to give him a running start, and easily caught the limb. Within seconds, he pulled himself up with a move Emily thought was reserved for stuntmen and gymnasts.

"Wow," Ginny whispered in awe. "He's like…a superhero."

"I think you're right, Ginny. And he'll have Duncan down from that tree in no time," Emily agreed with her niece as she watched Javy make his way from branch to branch until he reached Duncan. She heard a mix of voices, her nephew's childish whisper and Javy's low murmur in response.

Honestly, Emily's heart was pounding out of her chest as the top of the tree swayed and leaves rained down, and they decided to stop and chat. She bit her lower lip rather than call out, afraid she might startle either one of them.

The moment of male bonding over, Javy held out a hand. Duncan unhesitatingly reached out, and Emily felt something in her heart give way at the trust she saw in the little boy's face and the confidence she saw in Javy's. Slowly, he led the way down, guiding Duncan every step of the way until their feet—Javy's in black socks and Duncan's bare—hit solid ground.

Emily immediately scooped her nephew into a tight hug, as if she still needed to protect him now that he was safely on the ground. Relief quickly gave way to exasperation as she leaned back to meet Duncan's gaze. "You are in such big trouble, young man."

Exchanging glances with Javy, Duncan nodded. "I know."

Expecting a wealth of denials, Emily blinked in surprise. "You know?"

Her nephew nodded. "I should go back to the room now. Meggie's probably worried."

The words had barely left his mouth when a high-pitched female voice called out, "There you two are! Do you know how worried I've been?"

Meg, Aileen's longtime babysitter, ran toward them, worry and relief combining on her young face. "Emily, I am so sorry. I left the room for a few minutes to go get a drink from the soda machine. I thought Ginny and Duncan were still in the bedroom suite, watching a video. When I went to check on them and they weren't there…"

Her voice broke, and Emily wrapped an arm around the teenager's shoulders. "Everything's okay. Why don't you take them back to the room now? I'm sure they'll be more than willing to stay put now and finish that video," she said, pointedly meeting her niece's and nephew's gazes.

Ginny immediately nodded, but Duncan dropped his gaze to his bare feet. "I better not. I'm probably grounded and stuff for sneaking out."

Ginny reached out a sympathetic hand to her brother, and together they started back toward the hotel.

Meg turned to Emily with a puzzled frown. "Did Duncan just ground himself?"

Emily nodded. "I think so."

"Well, that's a first." Shaking her head, the babysitter thanked them for finding the kids before following her young charges back to the room.

Waiting until they disappeared inside the hotel, Emily turned to Javy. "Okay, what was that about?"

"What do you mean?"

"I mean, the whole talk in the treetop and Duncan forfeiting watching a video without anyone carrying him, kicking and screaming, away from the TV."

"Oh, that."

"Yes, that."

"It's a guy thing. I really don't think you'll understand," Javy said as he rolled down one of his shirtsleeves.

"Try me."

"It had to do with Duncan seeing his house from the treetop."

"He couldn't possibly. Aileen and Tom live almost twenty miles from here."

"Exactly. But sometimes a man has to take a chance, even if he knows he's reaching for the impossible."

He wasn't talking about her. She had no reason to think he was talking about her. But as Javy stepped closer, Emily caught her breath, unable to deny the single-minded focus in his gaze as he raised an arm, reached out and…took the jacket from her hands.

Embarrassed and hoping her breathless assumption hadn't been written on her face, Emily took a step back. Without his jacket to hold on to, her arms felt empty. She crossed, then uncrossed them before linking her fingers together in front of her.

"Thank you for, um, helping Duncan."

"It was nothing. Just a typical day in the life of a superhero."

Emily closed her eyes and counted to five, but when she opened them, Javy was still there. "You heard that, did you?"

"Yeah. Super hearing is just one of my superpowers."

"Along with your super ego," Emily muttered, trying to maintain an unaffected air when, in truth, she was as impressed as her six-year-old niece.

"There is that." He laughed as he hooked the jacket collar on two fingers and swung the jacket over his shoulder.

Catching sight of a long scratch marring his muscular forearm, Emily reacted without thinking. She stepped closer, ducking her head to try to see better. Taking his wrist in both her hands, she turned him more toward the light. "You're hurt."

After a brief pause, Javy said, "I'm fine."

"You need to get this cleaned out. There could be bits of bark caught in the cut. It could get infected."

"Emily."

She wasn't sure what exactly she heard in Javy's voice, but the sound was enough to make her realize how close they stood together. How his breath brushed the side of her face. How the muscles in his arms had turned to stone beneath her touch.

Helpless to resist, Emily looked up. With his dark hair and onyx eyes, he seemed a part of the night. Mysterious, cast in shadow and maybe even a little dangerous. His gaze dropped to her lips, and Emily swallowed hard. Make that a lot dangerous.

She should back up. Walk away. At the very least, make a joke to break the tension. But she'd never been good with jokes. She always forgot the punch lines. Until recently, when her own fiancé turned her into one.

If the recent memory of Todd's betrayal wasn't enough to slap her back to her senses, Emily flinched when light and laughter spilled out as a nearby door opened, a reminder that the reception was still going on and just about every person she knew was right inside the ballroom. If she thought the rumors about Todd were bad now, how much worse would it be if she were caught kissing another man at what should have been her wedding?

Jumping back, she said, "I have to go."

"Emily—"

"No, really. Thank you. For the dance, for helping Duncan, for…everything. But I have to go," Emily said as she backed away quickly.

Javy took a breath, looking ready to call after her, but she didn't dare let him stop her. She didn't know if she should blame heartache, and the loss of the wedding that should have been hers, or if something else was at fault, but Javier Delgado had an effect on her she couldn't explain. The kind of effect she'd never experienced before with any man.

He left her breathless, weak and far too vulnerable at a time when her heart was still raw.

As she raced away, she thought for a split second that Javy might come after her, but the tap of her heels was the only sound she heard. She could have cut through the ballroom, but she didn't think she could summon up one more fake smile. If the longer walk around the outside saved her from facing any more wedding guests, the blisters on her feet would be well worth it.

As she passed the French doors, she took a quick look inside, hoping to sneak by without being noticed. She shouldn't have worried. Inside, the reception was still going strong. A line of guests stood at the bar, and couples were twirling together to the romantic strains of a love song. No one even glanced her way or seemed to realize she was missing.

A dark-haired man spun his blonde partner into an elegant dip, and Emily's breath caught until the couple turned and she saw the man was not Javy. But just because she didn't see him on the dance floor, that didn't mean he hadn't gone back inside. Was he, right now, coaxing some other woman out of a corner and onto the dance floor?

Emily shook her head and started walking. She had to be crazy to be thinking of Javier Delgado now. To be thinking of him at all.

Emily and her parents were staying in a bungalow-style suite away from the main buildings of the hotel. She'd nearly reached the door to her room when she realized she'd left her purse and her key back by the tree her nephew had decided to climb.

She'd been in such a rush to get away from Javy—to run away from the undeniable and unexpected desire he sparked inside her—she'd foolishly forgotten the small clutch.

A sick feeling dragging down her stomach, Emily knew at

best she was going to have to go look for her purse. Worst-case scenario, she would have to go back into the ballroom to find one of her parents to let her in through one of their connecting rooms.

She'd let her guard down the moment she left the ballroom, unable to keep up that front a second longer, and she didn't know how she could possibly build it up enough to go back. Helplessness and frustration swamped her, and she leaned her forehead against the door, tempted to curl up in the doorway and cry.

"You forgot something."

Emily gasped and spun around at the sound of the deep murmur behind her. Javy stood a few feet away, his white shirt glowing in the faint light, her tiny beaded purse looking wholly out of place in his masculine hand. "My purse!"

The relief sweeping through her was out of proportion to the simple favor of returning her purse, but to Emily, Javy had just saved her from reentering the lion's den. The roller coaster of her emotions seemed to fly off track, and before she thought about what she was doing, she flung her arms around his neck.

"Oh, Javy, thank you!" The threat of tears choked her voice as she tried to explain. "I was so afraid I was going to have to go back to the ballroom, and I just didn't know how I could face all those people again—"

"You could do it," he murmured, his voice full of confidence. "You already faced them once, and the second time will only be easier. But it doesn't have to be tonight."

"Thanks to you." Emily pulled back to look up at him, a little embarrassed at how she'd thrown herself into his arms, but reluctant to leave all the same. Like the moment on the dance floor, where she forgot everything but the excitement, the anticipation, the seduction of being in his arms, she couldn't remember all the reasons why she shouldn't stay right where she was. "I guess a hero's work is never done. That's the second time you've come to the rescue."

"I'm returning your purse," he said wryly. "Seems more like a job for a Boy Scout than a superhero."

Emily's lips twitched until she could no longer hold back, and she wondered at his ability to make her laugh when she least felt like it. But Javy's own smile faded, his expression intensifying.

"There it is," he murmured.

"There…" She cleared her throat. "There what is?"

"A real laugh. I thought earlier you would be impossible to resist if you laughed."

"You did?"

"I did." Reaching up, he traced what was left of her smile with the pad of his thumb. "And you are."

Irresistible. The word certainly applied to Javy. What else could explain why Emily didn't protest as he slid his hand to the nape of her neck and pulled her closer? He moved purposefully—giving her time to notice the perfect shape of his mouth, time to feel the brush of his breath against her lips, time to escape…

But the slow, almost-relentless approach only built a pulse-pounding impatience, and instead of ducking away from his touch, Emily leaned into the kiss. The first barely there brush of his lips, and then the undeniable claim of his mouth over hers. She could taste a hint of the beer he'd had to drink earlier, and after a night filled with champagne toasts, it seemed so right. His kiss had an intoxication all its own, and the stars overhead seemed to spin wildly out of control.

Or maybe *she* was spinning out of control as Javy's hands slid down to her hips, each finger a brand against her flesh, even through the pale pink silk. She tightened her arms until her breasts pressed against the solid wall of his chest, but close wasn't close enough. Her shoulder blades bumped against the carved bungalow door, a sudden reminder that wove through her thoughts.

She'd hardly paid any attention to her room earlier—it was nice enough, but after all, it wasn't the honeymoon suite. Now, though, she could picture the room clearly with its dark wicker furniture, escape-to-the-tropics decor and large, empty bed.

The crazy thought of pulling the key from the purse Javy had returned and inviting him inside was so out of character, she should have been shocked. But all she felt was tempted by the wild impulse...

A faint, unfamiliar melody played through Emily's mind, too close to come from the ballroom, too far away to truly register. Javy broke the kiss, his breathing as uneven as hers. With the moon and light from the ballroom behind him, she couldn't see his expression, only the dark glitter of his eyes. He was so much more experienced than she at this kind of thing—then again, who wasn't?—did she dare hope he'd been as affected by their kiss?

"Sorry," he said, his voice a husky murmur as the sound repeated and Emily recognized the ring of a cell phone. "I don't know who would be calling me now."

Emily knew she should have been grateful for the interruption, but her still-pounding heart and tingling lips stomped out any other feeling beyond regret.

Fishing the phone out of his pocket, Javy frowned at the number displayed on the screen before answering with a rough "Yeah?" Emily could tell something was wrong even before he asked, "How bad is it?"

Agitation filled his steps as he started pacing while he listened to the person on the other end of the line. "Yeah, okay.

I'll be right there. Do me a favor and don't call Maria until I have a chance to take a look."

He snapped the phone closed and met Emily's gaze. "I have to go. A pipe burst at our restaurant. From what the night manager, Tommy, says, the place is a mess."

"Of course. I hope it's not as bad as it sounds."

Despite the barely restrained tension in the line of his jaw and the set of his shoulders, Javy hesitated, as if searching for something to say. A little surprised he didn't have a sexy quip ready even for a moment like this, Emily shook her head. It wasn't like she wanted to discuss their kiss or her unexpected desire to take things further than a kiss. She couldn't begin to explain it to herself.

"Go," she said softly.

"Emily..." His frustration was verbalized in a muttered curse—in Spanish—before he turned to walk away. He spun back around just as quickly. Catching her around the waist, he pulled her into his arms. He stole her breath and a quick, hard kiss before letting her go and backing away a second time.

"I'll call you," he promised.

Hugging her arms around the butterflies dancing in her stomach, Emily watched him disappear into the night. Maybe she was crazy, and maybe she was totally on the rebound after Todd's betrayal, but she suddenly wasn't sure she cared as long as Javy was the man to catch her.

Chapter Three

Javy hoped the restaurant wasn't as bad as he remembered. That after spending half the night wrestling with a Shop-Vac, feeling like he was trying to drain an ocean, he'd been too tired to clinically assess the damage. Sheer exhaustion must have made everything appear so much worse than it really was.

He was wrong.

The bathroom in which the pipe had broken and the area beyond showed the most damage. The force of the water had broken the concrete slab, cracking the Saltillo tile and flooding the place. He could see where the drywall had wicked water up a foot from the baseboards, darkening the paint like poorly done mountainscapes. The bathroom vanities were warped and waterlogged. Even some of the tables and chairs, with their elegant carving and colorful Mexican tile accents, showed signs of damage, a loss that hurt worst of all.

The harsh reality of day made the hours before seem even

more like a dream. Last night he'd held a beautiful woman in his arms. Then the clock had struck midnight and poof! He'd been up to his ankles in flood damage.

After all the hard work and worry about the restaurant, he should have collapsed into bed, grateful for the few hours of shut-eye. But memories of Emily's kiss had tortured him. He'd wanted to kiss her from the moment he spotted her at Kelsey and Connor's engagement party. He'd anticipated the challenge of cracking her cool veneer and drawing out the woman beneath. But he hadn't expected to experience the instant rush of heat and desire as Emily caught fire in his arms or to find himself in danger of getting burned.

Even when he'd finally drifted off to sleep, Emily had filled his thoughts. In his dreams, she'd stood right in front of him, but when he'd reached out, his arms had gone right through, and she'd disappeared.

Javy wasn't much for dream interpretation, but he did know he'd never had a woman he'd just met creep her way into his subconscious. Granted, Emily was stunning, but he'd dated his share of beauties—maybe even more than his share. Women who enjoyed the chase as much as he did and played by the same rules—all fun and games and no one got hurt.

He'd learned from his mistakes—and the one time he'd gotten in over his head and nearly drowned. But something about Emily was already pulling him deeper. He'd meant it when he'd called her brave. He couldn't think of another woman who would have painted on such a lovely smile and survived that wedding as a guest when she'd planned all along to be the bride. And the way she'd faced the cruel gossip with such class and grace…

He admired her, Javy realized suddenly, a word he hadn't figured he would associate with Emily Wilson. He'd assumed she was spoiled and selfish and would respond to her canceled wedding with a tantrum and a trip to Cannes or to some other rich-girl playground. She'd impressed him with a quiet composure and courage that threatened to get beneath his skin, and he wasn't sure he liked it.

So don't call her. It wasn't like he didn't have enough on his plate right now with the restaurant to repair. But he had the uneasy feeling that out of sight would not mean out of mind where Emily Wilson was concerned.

"It's bad, isn't it?"

Forcing his thoughts back to the restaurant, Javy turned to Tommy, the manager who'd discovered the burst pipe. He'd returned to Delgado's after realizing he'd lost his wallet sometime during his shift. Javy hated to think of the damage several more hours would have caused if he hadn't.

Yeah, it was bad, all right. Bad enough to bring back memories from ten years ago, when he lost his father, his fiancée and nearly lost the restaurant, as well. He could still remember the feelings of helplessness that had nearly overwhelmed him as everything he knew and loved threatened to disappear.

He'd been little more than a kid, so Javy supposed he should cut himself some slack, but he'd never forgiven himself for the fire that occurred on his watch.

At least now, the business and their finances were on firmer ground. He wouldn't need Connor to bail him out, and this time Javy wasn't the one at fault.

Focusing on the work to be done, he said, "We'll fix it. We'll have to shut down for a few days, but after that the restaurant will be up and running again."

He glanced over at the younger man, hoping to see some enthusiasm in the kid's expression. Instead, he was treated to a look of slack-jawed distraction. "Hey, kid, I'm giving one hell of pep talk here. Least you could do is pretend to listen."

"Yeah, um…what?" A slow flush climbed the younger

man's face, and Javy figured out why as soon as he heard the female voice behind him.

"I'm sorry. I didn't mean to interrupt."

Javy waited a second before he turned to face Emily Wilson. He knew damn well he'd look as besotted as Tommy if he didn't. The brief respite did little to prepare him. Kind of like no amount of time with your eyes closed could ever prepare you to look straight at the sun, Javy didn't think he could ever get used to Emily's breathtaking beauty.

The fancy gown, upswept hair and dramatic makeup from the night before were gone, replaced by a powder-blue camisole top, white capri pants and beaded sandals. A headband pushed back her golden blond hair, and only a hint of makeup kissed her face.

She probably thought she looked casual, but to Javy, she still looked classier than any woman he'd ever met. The low thrum of desire kicked up again, vibrating along every nerve in his body.

"I wanted to stop by and see if everything's okay. Obviously it's not," she said as she looked around the restaurant.

"It's going be. I was just telling Tommy, we'll be up and running in no time."

"Of course," she agreed faintly, a worried frown pulling her eyebrows at his pat response.

The compassion in her gaze caught him off guard, tugging at something in his chest and drawing out everything he wanted to deny, until a part of him longed to confess the feelings he'd buried since the moment he'd stepped inside the restaurant. That the damage left him heartsick; that he didn't know how long it would take before the place was up and running again; and that he worried that even then, the inevitable changes couldn't possibly live up to the way the restaurant had been before.

Emily lifted a hand to push her hair back from one shoulder, and the diamond bracelet she wore caught enough light to send prisms dancing across the restaurant. For a crazy second, Javy thought of the fake diamond engagement ring he'd bought for Stephanie.

Simulated, the salesgirl had called it. It had been all he could afford at eighteen, and as a symbol of his foolish teenage love, the diamond had been 100 percent genuine. But to Stephanie, the ring had been a cheap knockoff, and his best had been nothing but second rate.

Shoving aside memories—as well as any asinine thoughts of spilling his guts—he asked his young night manager, "Do me a favor, will you, Tommy? Move the damaged tables and chairs into the back, okay?"

Puzzled, the younger man asked, "Um, where do you want me to put them?"

"Just try to find some place out of the way."

As the younger man grabbed a carved chair in each hand, Javy turned back to Emily. He still wasn't sure why she'd come to the restaurant, but this definitely wasn't the way he wanted her to see it.

He was proud of his parents' place, of the hard work and dedication that had made Delgado's into a neighborhood landmark. He would have liked to show it to her at its best— on a Friday night, with the music blaring and every table filled by happy, hungry customers.

Not now, not like this, with the damp smell of stagnant water already replacing the restaurant's once mouthwatering aromas of peppers and spices, and with unwanted emotions and memories creeping past his defenses.

"What are you doing here, Emily?"

At his question, soft color slowly bloomed in her cheeks— like the petals of a rose unfolding. The effect was so beautiful and so stunning, he would have sworn she did it on purpose if he hadn't been pretty sure such a thing was impossible.

"I shouldn't have come. It was a mistake. I was thinking that I could help, but it's not like I can do—" she waved her free hand to encompass the mess around them "—anything."

Even without Emily's pronouncement, Javy would have bet the restaurant that major remodeling work was not her forte. That her experience was with hair dryers, not handsaws, and that the only nails she was familiar with were the ones painted a delicate pink on the tips of her fingers and toes.

But he also knew from listening to Connor moon over his girlfriend years ago that Emily could sing and dance. She'd been in dozens of beauty pageants and plays while growing up. That she was a skilled equestrian and had been an honor student. He could only imagine she'd honed those talents at college and in the years since.

Yet, for reasons he couldn't begin to imagine, she was ready to dismiss all that with the flick of a wrist to help him. The curiosity urging him to discover all the reasons why told Javy his mistake would be in asking her to stay.

In the end, he didn't have a chance to say anything. The front door opened, letting in a blast of heat and sunlight and a prayer in Spanish as his mother stepped into the restaurant. At work, she normally wore the same style dress as the rest of the female staff—a colorful blouse and embroidered skirt. It was strange to see her there dressed in a plain olive T-shirt and khaki pants. Her haste to leave the house showed in her hair, which she had left loose to fall to her waist. It had to be his imagination that overnight more gray seemed to shoot through the dark strands.

"Dios," Maria breathed, shock and dismay filling her expression.

"It's not as bad as it looks, Mama," Javy said immediately, not wanting to consider her reaction when she saw the worst of it.

"It's bad, Javier. Like the fire…"

Javy flinched at the reminder of his failure and the disaster that had almost destroyed them. "It isn't," he insisted. "It's not that bad. I can fix it…" His voice trailed off as for the second time, he lost his audience in the middle of his inspirational speech.

Maria stared at Emily, but unlike Tommy's wide-eyed infatuation, disapproval was written clearly on his mother's face. "*Solo tú,* Javier," she murmured. "Only you."

Realizing Maria was speaking Spanish to exclude Emily, he glanced at her, an apology in his eyes, and drew his mother aside. "Only me what, Mama?" he asked in English.

"Only you would bring a girl to the restaurant now. Bad enough you have a different girl in here every other week, but today? It is a disaster, and you bring a date."

His dating, or more specifically, his refusal to settle down, had long been a point of contention between them, one he refused to get into now. "We aren't on a date," Javy argued, but Maria would hear none of it.

"Do you think I do not recognize this girl? The one Connor was seeing all those years ago. The silly girl who did not think he was good enough for someone like her—"

"You're right." Emily stepped closer, covering the distance Javy had tried to put between them, and joined a conversation that she was smart enough to realize was about her. "I was a silly girl back then." Meeting Javy's gaze, she added in Spanish, *"Pero ahora mujer."*

Javy felt his jaw drop, and he ducked his head rather than let his mother see the smile he couldn't hold back. Muttering beneath her breath, Maria stalked off to the kitchen. As he met Emily's gaze, he let out a low laugh.

She winced. "I shouldn't have done that. I'm sorry—"

"Don't apologize." As much as he loved his mother, she was

a force to be reckoned with, and few people tried. He couldn't remember the last time anyone had silenced her. He never would have guessed Emily Wilson would be up for the job.

Once more she was showing him she was nothing like the spoiled rich girl he'd figured her for. She had spirit—buried deep, maybe, but still burning, despite what life had thrown at her. She'd shown it at the reception when she'd stood up to the gossips talking behind her back and just now with his mother.

But I am a woman now.

His mother had taught him Spanish straight from the cradle, so he certainly hadn't needed to think about translating the sentence Emily had spoken in perfect, if unaccented, Spanish. But it was as if his body had interpreted the words before his brain had even had the chance. Emily was a woman, no question about it. A fact both his body and his brain fully appreciated.

"You're incredible, you know that?"

She gave a questioning laugh. "Because I speak Spanish?"

"No, Emily, not because you speak Spanish."

Their gazes locked, and the low vibe of desire picked up speed until Javy half expected the windows to start shaking. Another wash of color lit Emily's cheeks. As incapable of accepting a compliment as she was at recognizing her own worth, she ducked her head and quickly explained, "Foreign language was a requirement at my school. My mother wanted me to take French, but my father thought Spanish more practical."

"I would have bet you spoke French."

"Well, I did take French my junior and senior year to make my mother happy. But my father was right about Spanish."

"So, you did what your father wanted, and you did what would make your mother happy," Javy said, seeing a pattern she had likely followed most of her life. "What about you, Emily? What do *you* want? What would make *you* happy?"

Emily glanced around the restaurant rather than focusing on Javy's questions. What *did* she want? Last night she'd come to the conclusion she wanted to see Javy again, to see if that quick start of excitement was due only to the emotions of the wedding, but now, with his restaurant in shambles, satisfying her curiosity seemed selfish.

Her breath caught when she turned back and nearly bumped into him. He'd moved closer as she focused on the damage, and now stood mere inches away. Dark circles lined his eyes, and a hint of beard shadowed his jaw, evidence of the first of many long nights and the hard work ahead.

"I want…" *You,* she thought, the fluttering in her belly proof of the unspoken words. But of course, she couldn't admit that. She'd tried telling herself her rash and reckless behavior was nothing more than a reaction to her former fiancé's betrayal. But she'd been unable to push aside the thought that last night had far more to do with Javier Delgado than it did with Todd.

After all, during their engagement, Todd had kissed her good-night countless times, and not once had Emily given in to the urgency to take that kiss beyond a bedroom doorway. Like their wedding, their wedding night was to have been perfectly arranged, a night filled with flowers, candles and champagne. But all the romantic staging in the world couldn't add what Javy's kiss had shown her had been missing from her relationship with Todd—unplanned, unstaged, undeniable desire.

Admitting that to herself was bad enough; admitting it to Javy would be giving him an advantage he didn't need.

"I, um, want to hear more about how you're going to fix the restaurant," she said lamely, recalling the conversation she'd interrupted when she first arrived.

Javy didn't immediately respond, and Emily reminded herself that his dark eyes couldn't possibly see the thoughts bouncing wildly through her brain…or the desire doing a far more seductive slide through her body. She wasn't entirely sure she believed it, though, and was relieved when he finally answered.

"Most of it will be cleanup and demolition before I can move on to the repairs. And…"

His voice trailed away as he looked around, and he dug his hands into the back pockets of his faded jeans, showing an uncertainty she hadn't seen in him before. This other side, this shy, almost boyish side charmed whatever small part of her that hadn't already been won over by his confident, almost cocky attitude.

"I'd like to do some remodeling." He shrugged. "As big of a disaster as this is, it would be the perfect opportunity. We'll have to close down while we make the repairs, so why not make some improvements, as well?"

"Like what?"

He waved a hand to a doorway off the main dining area. "We need to upgrade the bar. Make it into more of a sports lounge. Add some flat-screen TVs, couple of pool tables, electronic dartboards. It's way too small right now, but we could steal space from the patio. Of course, that would mean building a new outdoor area, but there's room if we take away a small section of the parking lot. It would be a lot of work but…"

"You could do all that? Tear down walls and everything?"

"Tearing 'em down is easy. Building them back up takes a little more skill. But I have a cousin who works construction. I know Alex would want to be in on the job. And the staff here… They could help out with trips to the hardware store and hauling supplies. That would make a big difference."

Emily thought the biggest difference would be keeping his employees involved while the restaurant was closed and they were otherwise out of work. But judging by the casual way he spoke, Javy wasn't looking for praise.

"Seems like you've given this a lot of thought," she offered, although he didn't sound as excited as she would have expected.

He gave a short laugh. "Probably more than I should. Maria isn't big on change. I know she'll want everything back the way it was…like nothing ever happened." Despite the easy grin he flashed her, the spark in his dark eyes when he talked about the remodeling had faded.

"I'm sure if you talked to your mother about it, you could change her mind. You could convince her that it will be better than before."

His handsome features twisted with a wry smile. "There is no better than before."

Emily wondered what he meant by that, but his cell phone rang and, after a quick apology, he started talking to the insurance company before she had a chance to ask.

As Javy walked into the back office in search of a policy number, Emily took a moment to focus on the restaurant instead of on the damage. A series of photographs covering a wall of the front lobby caught her eye and helped her see beyond the disarray to how the place looked on a typical busy night. Some of the pictures had the faded yellow tint of age, but even without that telltale sign, she could have guessed the timeline by the fashions. She smiled at the sight of large mustaches, feathered hair and bell-bottoms.

In more recent shots, she could almost feel the energy pulsing from the vibrant pictures that caught waiters and waitresses with loaded trays as they ducked between crowded tables filled with laughing patrons. In a few of the frames, she spotted Javy. He wore what she assumed was the typical male uniform, a white button-down shirt and black pants, a sharp contrast to the colorful shirts and embroidered, tiered skirts worn by the waitresses.

His heart-stopping grin was on display in almost every shot, and she tried not to notice the interchangeable women by his side. Blonde, brunette, redhead, he didn't seem to have a type, except the women had one thing in common—they were all beautiful.

Last night Emily had lain awake for hours, reliving the memory of Javy's kiss even as she strictly told herself to forget it—to forget *him*. He had a reputation as a playboy, and that kiss had proved he had the skills to match. She'd be foolish to walk any further down a road that would only lead to heartbreak. But the more she argued how dangerous Javy was, the more…safe he started to seem.

Oh, by three o'clock in the morning she'd convinced herself she was suffering from sleep deprivation. But even at six, after a few hours of sleep, the idea still circled through her thoughts. Todd had hurt her when he'd cheated and lied and pretended to be something he wasn't. He'd fooled her every step of the way.

But with Javy, her eyes were wide-open. She knew what he was and what he wasn't, and she had no expectations beyond that. No plans of becoming a permanent fixture by his side in future photos. And as long as she kept that in mind, she had little chance of getting hurt.

She had her own safety still firmly in mind as she wandered around the back of the restaurant, toward the bar and patio. When she caught sight of Maria through the sliding-glass doors, Emily immediately froze. Still stunned by the way she'd stood up to the older woman, Emily doubted she had it in her to go another round. But Maria wasn't paying any attention to her. With the blazing summer sun outside, Emily doubted she could even be seen inside, and Maria's attention was firmly fixed on the tables and chairs Javy had asked Tommy to move out of the way.

Emily was ready to slip away unnoticed when she saw Javy walk over to his mother, bend down and urge her to stand.

"Another piece of my Miguel…gone. Soon there will be nothing left." The words were muffled by the glass, but Emily could hear the devastating sense of loss in Maria's voice.

"That's not true. You still have the restaurant, you have your memories and nothing can take him from your heart." Despite Javy's encouragement, sorrow still pulled at his mother's expression, and he quickly promised, "And I can fix the chairs and tables. I can cut away the worst of the damage, sand down the tables and chairs and restain them—"

"It won't be the same, *hijo.*"

Maria was too focused on the furniture to see the expression on her son's face, but Emily couldn't pull her gaze away from the pain of rejection written across his handsome features. She wasn't going to be any good at protecting herself, after all. She already cared enough to hurt *for* Javy. Did she really think she could keep her heart from breaking because of him?

Emily made her way back to the main dining area without Javy or his mother spotting her, and that was where he found her minutes later. "Hey, sorry that took so long," he offered, his manner completely at ease, but Emily knew better.

She could still see the rejection he was trying to hide in the tension in his jaw and the faint lines between his eyebrows. If not for that brief scene she'd witnessed, Emily might not have noticed. But now she couldn't *not* see it.

"Is everything okay?" she asked, even though she knew the answer he would give.

"Yeah, it's fine. Insurance is a hassle, but we'll get through."

But it won't be the same. Maria's words seemed to echo in the dining room, and Emily didn't doubt Javy could hear them, too.

No wonder he'd been reluctant to talk about his idea for the restaurant, already knowing how his mother would respond. Emily longed to give back a little of the confidence he'd given her when he took her hand and led her to the dance floor. But how could she say anything without revealing that she'd overheard their conversation?

Without words to use, she lifted a hand. She brushed her fingertips along the lines on his forehead before pressing her hand to his jaw. The scrape of his beard against her palm sent shivers racing up her arm and scattered goose bumps across her chest, as if he'd trailed that whisker-roughened skin across her flesh... His eyes darkened with desire, and Emily almost forgot why she'd touched him in the first place—other than for the sheer pleasure of touching him at all.

"I know you will," she said softly. And maybe it wouldn't be the same, but she sensed how important it was that he at least try—for his own sake and for his father's memory. If only she knew how to convince him...

Lifting his hand, he wrapped his fingers around her wrist and slid her palm slowly from his jaw, across his chin, until his lips pressed into the center of her sensitized flesh. "You sound pretty sure about that." She felt the heat of his breath and the words he spoke against her palm, a seductive sign language she had little trouble translating.

Forcing herself to concentrate, she said, "Maybe because I'm pretty sure about you."

"But you haven't even seen what I can do yet."

Emily swallowed. "I think you can do anything you put your mind to."

For instance, he could seduce her into forgetting everything, even the goal she had of trying to convince him to work on the furniture. And although playing with fire was safer than digging deeper into long-buried memories, a hint of disappointment that he wouldn't confide in her lingered beneath the desire.

Except there wasn't supposed to be anything but desire, Emily was trying to remind herself when Javy lowered their still-joined hands. His dark lashes fell, hiding his gorgeous eyes for a second, but not before she caught a glimpse of the helplessness she'd seen when he spoke to his mother.

He ran his free hand along the carved back of one of the nearby chairs. "My dad made this furniture. He worked on it in his free time, so it took months before he could replace the old pieces with ones that were uniquely his."

"Your father was very talented."

"I don't know how many times he tried to show me how he carved every leaf, every flower. It took forever, and the restaurant already had a bunch of tables and chairs, and I wanted to be out playing with my friends. I just didn't get it, and after a while, he gave up." A muscle in his jaw clenched, and Emily could sense he was talking about more than learning his father's craft—almost as if he felt his father had given up on *him*.

"Javy—"

"And now it's too late," he interrupted. "So, you're wrong, Emily. I can't fix this."

Maybe it was too late to resolve whatever conflict had existed between Javy and his father, but Emily felt the slow burn of anger that Maria couldn't see how important it was for Javy to do this for her, for his father's memory, for *himself.* How could she simply brush all that aside?

Despite the finality of his words, he wouldn't have made the offer unless he *could* do something to repair the furniture. It was his mother's lack of faith, not his lack of ability, that was holding him back, and Emily simply couldn't let it end there.

"How do you know?" she challenged.

"What?"

"How do you know you can't until you try? What was it you told me last night? No more standing on the sidelines. Right?"

A slow smile kicked up the corners of his mouth, but more than practiced seduction backed the expression as a hint of light rekindled in his eyes. "You think it's time to dance?"

If her heart had any say in the matter, it was time to do the samba, the tango, and a little salsa dancing, as well, as long as Javy was her partner. Caught up in the moment, Emily said, "You should talk to your mother about remodeling the restaurant, too."

Javy's grin faded away, and he shook his head. He pulled his hand from hers, and Emily tried not to see the move as a rejection. "She'll never go for it. Believe me. It's her place, and it's her call."

"Her place?" Emily echoed. "And what? You just work here?"

"Something like that."

Emily didn't believe it for a moment. "Javy—"

"Look, Emily, my mother doesn't want to make any changes, and it's better to just let it go."

"Better? Or easier? Because, believe me, I know all about doing things the easy way." During the long night, when she hadn't been thinking of Javy, she'd had plenty of time to face some less than flattering facts. "I almost got *married* because everyone told me how perfect Todd was and how happy we'd be. It was easier to believe they were right than to take a stand and tell my entire family they were wrong."

"That's hardly the same thing," he argued, brushing by her as if the last few moments had never happened.

"Of course it's not the same. I seriously doubt you would have accepted Todd's proposal no matter what my family said," she retorted, earning a dark look that he probably thought would scare her off but only made her that much more determined.

Catching his arm, she had to remember to focus on what she was saying instead of on the warm skin and muscle beneath her palm. "You know the restaurant will be better with those changes," she said softly. "If it's a matter of money, I can—"

Jerking away from her touch as violently as if she'd stuck him with a red-hot fork, Javy snapped, "No."

Emily had known she'd risk offending his ego when she offered the money, but she hadn't expected such an abrupt refusal. "Won't you even consider—"

"No, Emily. Forget it. I've taken all the money from your family that I'm going to in this lifetime."

Taken money? "What are you talking about? How could you take money from my family? You don't even *know* my family."

But as the anger faded from his expression, replaced with a look of guilt and regret, Emily realized this was no misunderstanding. Javy knew exactly what he was talking about, and she wasn't going to like hearing it. A muttered curse beneath his breath confirmed her fear.

"I'm sorry, Emily. I thought…I thought you knew." He reached out a hand, and this time she was the one to pull back.

"Knew what? Tell me. All of it," she demanded despite the uneasy churning in her stomach, unwilling to be appeased by less than the truth.

Sympathy shone in Javy's dark eyes, an emotion Emily was far too familiar with. "Your family paid Connor to stop seeing you all those years ago. That's why he left town. He figured you were never going to go with him, so he took the money…and gave it to my family."

Chapter Four

Color faded from Emily's face, leaving behind a vulnerability etched in her delicate features. Javy swore beneath his breath. He could have kicked himself for blurting out what he hadn't realized until then was a secret.

"Connor gave us the money to save the restaurant after a fire destroyed the kitchen. I'm sorry, Emily," he repeated. He'd had no right to attack her when she'd only been trying to help. When she'd been…

Right, his conscience taunted, but he thrust the thought aside. Emily didn't understand. The restaurant was his mother's heart and soul, her last, best tie to her husband. Making changes or *not* making changes was up to her.

And even though Javy wished she trusted in him, she didn't. At least not the way she had in his father.

Not the way Emily believed in *him.*

He'd seen the faith and confidence glowing in her eyes, and

it warmed something deep inside his chest, lighting fire to the dreams he'd been denying. But hadn't he learned already that dreams were like quicksand? Seemingly real and solid on the surface, but completely unable to bear the weight of reality? He'd had too many dissolve beneath his feet.

And Emily Wilson, with her turquoise eyes and glorious golden hair, was as much of a dream as anyone he'd ever met. But it was the way she got under his skin, the way she made him want to believe in something *more,* that made her so seductive—and so dangerous.

But none of that was her fault. He had no excuse for treating her the way he had, and she had every right to be backing toward the door away from him. "Emily, wait."

"I have to go."

She slipped out the door before he could stop her, but he caught up with her outside. Midmorning sunlight rode a wave of heat, blasting them both, and Javy squinted against the glare. "At least let me apologize."

"There's no need," she insisted as she slid her purse strap over one shoulder. Looking as cool and remote as some Hollywood glamour girl from the past, she added, "You didn't do anything."

Then why did her casual absolution make him feel that much worse?

"Look, I don't blame you for being pissed off."

"I'm not. Really," she insisted, and Javy could see she was telling the truth. A shadow of hurt lingered, but none of the fury he'd expected. "What would be the point?"

"The point?" he echoed. "The point is to yell and scream and let it all out until you feel better."

Emily sighed. "I'm fine, Javy. That was years ago. Connor was right. I had already made up my mind that our relationship was moving too fast and that I wasn't ready to run off with him. I'm not surprised he gave the money to your family.

That's the kind of friend he is. Now he and Kelsey are completely in love, and everything has worked out for the best, so why bother getting upset?"

"Because none of that changes the fact that your family went to Connor behind your back, and they kept it a secret all these years, until some loudmouthed jerk threw it in your face when you were only trying to help."

Her lips twitched in what he thought might be a real smile, but she ducked her head before he could tell for sure. "I happen to like that loudmouthed jerk, so that makes it hard to be angry with him."

"Yeah, well, the jerk likes you, too, and he'd feel better if you did get angry, seeing how he deserves it."

"You don't, and I'm glad you told me. It makes me feel better about the decision I've made."

"What decision?"

"I want to move out of my parents' house."

Javy's eyebrows rose in surprise. "Are you sure you don't want to think about that first?"

"I have been thinking about it. This isn't about what happened with Connor. Obviously, I was going to move in with Todd after the wedding. I don't see why all my plans should change simply because my fiancé ended up being a liar and a cheat."

Afraid she might be getting in over her head, Javy said, "You know, there's no hurry. I'm sure your parents—"

"My parents would gladly let me stay at home, where I can be the little girl they'll do anything to protect." A hint of bitterness underscored her words, telling Javy she wasn't as ambivalent about her parents' inference as she'd like to believe. "I want to do this. I *need* to."

"Okay, but you don't have to do it all by yourself. I have a cousin…" Catching sight of the look on her face, he laughed.

"Yeah, I've got a lot of cousins. Anyway, Anna's a real estate agent. I'll introduce you, and she can show you a listing of houses for sale."

"Thank you," she said, her sigh of relief revealing her doubts about doing this all on her own.

And she wouldn't be alone. He'd be on hand to help. Despite the fact that he'd be working like a madman in a few days to get the restaurant back in running shape, he'd be there for Emily.

You've never stuck with anything in your whole life.

The echo of his father's long-ago accusation rang through his mind, and Javy locked his jaw against the memories. If he had to slow down time, he'd figure out a way. The Wilsons' payoff had helped his family but had ultimately hurt Emily. He owed it to her to do what he could do to make things right. And they owed it to themselves to see where the undeniable chemistry led.

It didn't matter if he couldn't make things *stick.*

Emily had just escaped from one serious tangle and was looking for even more freedom. No way would she be interested in getting tied up in a long-term relationship again.

Relaxing with the thought, he said, "Hey, you're welcome. But I haven't even done anything yet."

"That's not true. You're the first person to ask me what I want and what would make me happy. You've given me a lot to think about, and finding my own place is definitely one of the things I want."

After giving him her number so he could call when his cousin was available to meet them, Emily climbed into her car. She pulled out of the parking lot, but not before glancing back. Their gazes met, and Javy would have sworn the sweat beading at his temples and the heat shimmering across the twenty feet of asphalt between them had nothing to do with the hundred-plus temperature and everything to do with the spark and sizzle of that momentary connection.

In the end, it was Emily who looked away first. She turned onto the street and drove off, but as he'd suspected, out of sight did not equal out of mind, and her last lingering look left Javy wondering about all the other things Emily Wilson might want.

Emily made it a little more than a mile before she pulled off into a grocery store parking lot. Her hands were clenched on the steering wheel as Javy's words echoed through her thoughts.

Your family paid Connor to stop seeing you all those years ago. That's why he left town.

Humiliation burned her cheeks. Nearly ten years removed from her family's manipulation, the betrayal shouldn't have stung so badly. Except Emily wasn't sure anything had changed. If she fell for the wrong man now, how would her parents react? Would they trust her to make the right decision, or would they go behind her back and stack the odds for a favorable outcome?

I've taken all the money from your family that I'm going to in this lifetime.

She wished Javy's words didn't mean so much to her. After all, he wasn't saying he cared about her more than her family's money, only that he wouldn't accept financial help. Not exactly the same thing. His words were a declaration of pride, not an outpouring of emotion.

When her cell phone rang, Emily reached for her purse, grateful for the distraction until she saw her sister's number on the screen. She was surprised Aileen had waited this long to call. "Hello, Aileen."

"Emily! We missed you this morning."

Her family had made plans to have breakfast before checking out of the hotel, but most of the talk would center on the wedding, and she'd had enough. "I left word at the restaurant that I wasn't going to make it."

"I know. The maître d' told us you weren't coming, but of course, he couldn't tell us *why.*"

Emily sighed. "I just needed some time alone."

"*All* alone?" Aileen stressed.

Emily shook her head. She loved her sister, but the woman was anything but subtle. Still, that didn't mean Emily would make it easy on her. "What do you mean?"

"One minute you're dancing with the best man, and the next minute you've both left the reception."

And of course, Aileen would have heard all about what had happened after the reception. Some babysitters might have tried to keep the kids' escape a secret, but Meg wasn't the type to lie. Just as well, since Emily doubted anything would have kept Ginny quiet when it came to a "superhero" rescuing her little brother.

"What exactly do you think happened, Aileen?"

"I don't know." A sly note entering her voice, her sister said, "That's what I'm calling to find out."

"*Nothing* happened," Emily insisted, keeping the amazing kiss to herself. "Except for the part about Duncan getting stuck in the tree."

"Well, I'm proud of you for going to the wedding, and I hope you'll be able to put this behind you and move on."

"That is my plan," Emily agreed, thinking of her decision to move and find her own place.

"Speaking of plans, Mother has a dinner party in the works. Dad's thinking of asking Dan Rogers to become a partner in the business."

"He's… Really?"

Good thing she'd already pulled over. Emily wasn't sure how many more unexpected announcements she could take in one day.

"You sound surprised," Aileen ventured carefully.

"Aren't you?" Emily questioned. "Doesn't this whole thing seem too fast?"

"Well, no. You know Dad wants to cut back his hours and start an early semiretirement. He's been talking about bringing in a partner for months."

"I know." Her father had gold starred Todd for that position. The wedding would have been not only a "welcome to the family" but also a welcome to the family business. With Todd out of the picture, her father was still moving forward, substituting Plan B, in the form of Dan Rogers.

And what about you? What are you doing with Javier Delgado?

It's not the same, she argued, with the annoying voice poking guilty needles in her conscience. And okay, kissing a guy on the day she was supposed to have married another man might have some shades of Plan B, but Emily wasn't going to *marry* Javy.

Everything Emily knew about him told her he was the last man to want to get married, and as long as she kept that firmly in mind, that made him just about perfect.

Half an hour later Emily pulled up to her parents' circular driveway. A familiar brown delivery truck blocked access to the four-car garage on the side of the sprawling Scottsdale home. She cut the engine and climbed from her car as a uniformed man circled the back of the truck. The door was rolled up, revealing dozens of boxes in every shape and size, and the driver had three packages stacked high in his arms.

Packages he'd clearly carried *away* from the house.

A combination of humiliation and anger wrestled inside Emily, twisting and turning until she didn't know which emotion was winning.

"Oh, hi." Looking at her from over the top of a box, he

rushed to put the packages down. Emily didn't know what the guy saw in her face, but he immediately said, "Give me two seconds and I'll move the truck."

"Is that the last of the packages?" Emily asked.

"Nah, there's like a ton more, but I'm blocking the way and—"

"It's all right," she insisted. "I can park here for now."

The front door was open, revealing a travertine foyer crowded by various boxes waiting to be sent back. Only days before Emily had watched as those packages arrived, one after the other, and she'd tried to guess what might be inside, like a kid in the days leading up to Christmas.

She didn't remember when she stopped believing in Santa, but she'd been just as foolish to believe in happily ever after.

"Don't forget to…" Charlene Wilson strode into the foyer, only to stop short when she saw her daughter. "Oh, Emily. I didn't realize you were back already."

Emily thought a look of uneasiness crossed her mother's features, but it was hard to tell. Wearing tan slacks and a copper-colored silk blouse that complemented her brown hair and eyes, Charlene Wilson was as composed as always. Emotional outbursts were unacceptable in her world.

Yell and scream and let it all out until you feel better.

Emily wondered what her mother would do if she took Javy's advice—if she yelled, screamed or even so much as raised her voice. She couldn't imagine Charlene's response. But when Emily realized she couldn't picture herself actually *doing* any of those things, a feeling of discontent swept through her.

What was so wrong with real, honest emotion? Why did she feel as if she'd spent her whole life covering up…when she didn't even know what she had to hide?

"I was planning to return the wedding gifts myself," she

told her mother stiffly as the driver came back inside and piled his arms high once more.

Waffle maker, she guessed as he picked up the first rectangle. Good thing it was going back. She loved waffles, and in the mood she was in, she'd likely eat forty-seven. Each and every one topped with whipped cream and powdered sugar.

"There's no need for you to worry about it," her mother was saying.

She would have hated doing it, Emily admitted. Every word she wrote to the people kind enough to send gifts would have made her feel more of a fool and a failure. And yet... "I said I would."

"And now you don't have to, Emily. It's been taken care of."

Just like her parents had taken care of everything. Everything she didn't want to deal with and, in the case of Connor McClane, everything *they* hadn't wanted to deal with. They'd done such a good job taking care of her, she'd missed out on the growing pains, where she was supposed to learn to take care of herself.

It was on the tip of her tongue to ask her mother about the money they'd paid Connor to leave town. About the money they'd *wasted,* since she never would have had the guts to run away with Connor, anyway.

But then Javy's face flashed in her mind, his obvious love for his family's restaurant shining in his dark eyes, and she reminded herself that things happened for a reason.

Taking a deep breath, Emily said, "Thank you, Mother."

"You're welcome," Charlene said as she led the way toward the living room.

Emily always thought her mother had exceptional taste. It showed throughout the house, the living room being no exception. The rich green and beige tones of the couches were a perfect match for the gold-hued coffee and end tables. The floor-to-ceiling slate fireplace was the focal point of the room, although Emily couldn't recall it ever being used, and a family portrait hung above the mantle.

The photographer had captured Emily's perfect smile with the flash of his camera, but for the first time, Emily noticed how the smile never reached her eyes. For all the years of practice, she hadn't gotten that part right.

"Did Aileen get in touch with you?" her mother asked.

"She did."

"Good. I'm going to need your help with the dinner party."

Emily turned away from the portrait as her mother took a seat on the couch. "My help?"

"Yes, it wouldn't hurt for you to be more involved in your father's business."

Thinking that deciding on appetizers and selecting entrées would hardly help her father, Emily nonetheless said, "All right. I'll help."

"Good." Charlene nodded in satisfaction, leaving Emily with the feeling she would regret her far-too-easy capitulation.

Later that evening, after swimming a dozen or so laps in the Olympic-size pool in the backyard, Emily lounged in a chaise. The outdoor lights highlighted the pool's rock waterfall and the surrounding queen palms, but Emily had long ago aimed a few of the lights in her direction.

She loved the peace and quiet of the outdoors at night, even in the warmest months. Most evenings she paged through fashion magazines or read a romance novel, but tonight neither appealed. Instead, a legal notepad rested on her bare legs, and she chewed on the end of a pen as she pondered the list in front of her. A single line divided the fourteen-inch page, and each side had a heading. On the left, the words "What makes you happy?" On the right, "What do you want?"

So far, both sides were pathetically blank. She'd mentally run through her many hobbies and the dozens of activities she'd participated in over the first twenty-eight years of her life. From the pageants to the plays, to the ballet and ball-rooms, she couldn't help feeling she'd done all of it to make other people happy. Her parents, her teachers, her coaches.

She'd fallen into a habit of doing what was expected, of coloring inside the lines. And as much as she'd love to turn the world upside down, to live life like a Picasso, the page in front of her remained blank, except for the rigid, straight lines slicing across the paper.

Ripping off the sheet, she crumpled the paper with both hands and tossed it aside. She then turned the legal pad on its side. She drew a new centerline and rewrote the headings against the grain.

"What do I want?" she asked out loud. The splash of the waterfall echoed her question but offered no response.

Javy's face flashed in her mind—his dark eyes and sexy smile. A small shiver raised goose bumps over her arms and legs, despite the ninety-plus–degree weather.

She lowered her pen, and the tip hovered over the right column. Tightening her grip, she moved the pen to the left side and wrote his name.

Coward, her conscience mocked.

You're the bravest woman I've ever met. The memory of Javy's deep voice blended with the buzz of the cicadas in a nearby tree.

Straightening her back, she drew a definitive line across his name and moved the scrolling calligraphy to the right side, a feeling of satisfaction and anticipation coming over her with each letter she wrote.

Emily jumped as her cell phone rang. She normally left it inside when she went out to swim, and she had brought it out for only one reason. Her heartbeat picking up as she flipped it open, she said, "Hello?"

"Emily? It's Javy."

"Hi. That was fast."

His low chuckle sent another round of goose bumps racing over her skin. "Fast? Sweetheart, I haven't considered calling a girl moving fast since I was in second grade."

Staring at his name written across the page, Emily wondered if she wasn't the one moving too fast. Refusing to chicken out before she'd, well, crossed the road, Emily said, "I, um, thought you might be calling because you'd talked to your cousin."

"I know. I was only teasing. I did talk to Anna, although I would have called you tonight even if I hadn't. Just to make sure you're all right."

His concern washed over her, and Emily drew her knees closer to her chest, as if she could somehow keep this quivering feeling of anticipation trapped inside. "I'm fine," she said, even as the toll of a long day threatened to sink her spirits.

He was silent so long, Emily began to wonder if she'd lost the connection. Finally, though, he sighed and said, "I hate to tell you, Emily, but you're a terrible liar."

Opening her mouth in denial, she gave a soft, guilty laugh instead. "I know. I always have been. Just as well. It keeps me honest."

"Now, if there was only a way to make sure everyone else did the same."

After Todd's betrayal, and even her parents' and Connor's lies of omission, Emily had certainly had her share of people deceiving her, but she didn't think Javy was talking about her life. This was about him, about his past. "I guess there are no guarantees, but not every woman lies, Javy."

He fell silent again, this time in surprise, but he rebounded quickly. "Would a man who loves women as much as I do ever say such a thing?"

He might not have said it, but Emily didn't doubt for a second that a woman had lied. A long time ago, most likely, judging by his well-established trend of girl hopping.

Who was it? she wondered but didn't ask the question, knowing he wouldn't answer. And feeling absurdly hurt by it.

He knew what had happened with Todd. How her fiancé had cheated and gotten another woman pregnant. How Todd had asked her to marry him only to try and save face with his wealthy family.

And he knew how her parents had paid Connor to stop seeing her. Her pathetic love life was as open as a tabloid magazine, and yet she knew nothing about Javy's beyond the shallow relationships he juggled to keep anyone from looking deeper.

Focusing on the right-hand heading, Emily reminded herself that she didn't need to know Javier Delgado's life story to be happy, and she'd just as soon he forget all about hers. Just like, had he known she'd witnessed it, he would want her to forget about the longing for approval she'd seen in his eyes when he talked to his mother.

This is about having fun, not getting serious, she mentally instructed herself. Javy was a sexy, charming flirt with no interest in settling down. The reasons why didn't matter. All that she cared about was that he was sexy and charming and flirting with her.

"Of course you never said something like that," she finally responded. "But I think it has more to do with fear of your mother than it does with your love of women. My guess is Maria wields one heck of a spatula."

"Ha! I can totally take on her spatula. It's the cast-iron skillets and butcher knives that have me shaking in my shoes," he said wryly. "As soon as the restaurant's back in business, you've got to taste her enchiladas. They are to die for."

"I can't wait," Emily agreed, absurdly happy with the invitation.

"I'm afraid you'll have to. It's gonna be a few weeks until the place is in working order again."

And maybe *that* was what made Emily happiest of all. That she would still be seeing Javy weeks from now...

"I'll be there," she promised. "The very first night you reopen."

"Hey, that's not a bad idea."

"What isn't?"

"Having a grand reopening. We'll turn it into a party so everyone will know the construction is over."

Excitement filled his voice. How much more excited would he be if the grand reopening included showcasing a new bar and patio area? But she would leave that argument for another time. For now she said, "That sounds perfect."

Javy talked for another minute about some of the specials they could offer, as well as advertising the event and booking entertainment. Turned out he had yet another cousin in a local cover band.

"But don't think that all of this has made me forget."

"Forget what?" she asked.

"That something's got you down."

"It's nothing, really, and talking to you has already made me feel one hundred percent better."

"I'm flattered, but not distracted. Tell me what's wrong. Is it because of what I told you?"

Not bothering to lie, she admitted, "That is part of it. I'm still trying to sort out how I feel about what my parents did."

"What did they say?"

"What?"

"When you talked to them about it… You *did* talk to them, didn't you, Emily?"

"Well, no. I thought about it but—"

"What would be the point?" he said, filling in the blanks.

"Exactly," she said, feeling defensive without completely knowing why.

"Emily." She expected to hear a hint of chiding in his tone, a grown-up talking to a stubborn child, but she heard only sincerity and the same concern she'd hugged to her heart seconds ago. "You need to talk to them. Okay, so everything worked out for the best, but they couldn't have known that back then. They hurt you with their lack of trust, and you should tell them that."

"I'm not sure how you think that conversation would go, but I don't think it would end the way you think," she said with a huffing laugh.

"How do *you* think it would end?"

"With them telling me they know what's best and me thanking them for looking out for me."

He made a soft sound, half laughing, half swearing. "You're not kidding, are you?"

"I'm afraid not. It's pretty much what happened this afternoon." After giving him a quick rundown of the gift-return debate, she said, "You probably think I'm a spoiled brat. I didn't want to be the one to return the gifts, but I didn't want my mother to do it, either."

"Of course you didn't *want* to do it. Returning wedding gifts is a job that pretty much sucks on all sides," he said, startling a laugh out of her at the unexpected phrasing. "But it was your responsibility, and your mother didn't have a right to take that from you."

A personal note entered Javy's voice, and Emily would have bet he was thinking of the restaurant and his mother's refusal to let him make changes. Even though they'd met only days ago, they had more in common than she would have believed given the differences in their backgrounds.

And not once had he hinted that maybe, just maybe, Emily had purposely hesitated in sending back the gifts, hoping her parents would take care of the difficult matter for her.

"Thank you, Javy."

Emily didn't know if he heard the huskiness in her voice, but his response was purposefully light as he said, "Nothing I like better than a beautiful woman in my debt."

"Well, you'll have my undying gratitude if you called to tell me your cousin can show me some available houses tomorrow."

"I did, and she can."

Emily barely muffled a squeal of delight. "That is perfect. I can hardly wait. Thank you!"

"Hey, don't thank me yet!"

"Why? Why not?" Her hand tightened on the phone. Did he foresee some kind of problem with his cousin showing her the houses?

A hint of seduction crept into his tone. "Because I like it so much better when you thank me in person."

Heat pooled in her belly at the promise in his words.

Chapter Five

Late the next afternoon Javy stood in the middle of the restaurant, waiting for Anna and Emily. It had been his cousin's idea to meet there. Anna hadn't seen the damage to the restaurant yet and wanted to come by, supposedly to lend moral support. Javy was pretty sure what she wanted was to give him advice on redecorating.

He'd spent the day ripping up baseboards and pulling away the crumbling drywall. A plumber had repaired the busted pipe, but it would be another two days before someone could fix the concrete slab. Once that was done, demoing the cracked tiles would be the next major project. And since it would be impossible to match what had been installed years ago, he'd already decided to tear up the dining area, as well as the baths and hallway.

He'd talked to his cousin Alex, who had promised to have a crew on hand, ready and willing to work double-time. The sooner the job was completed, the sooner Maria would see that Javy had made the right decision.

And what about the rest of the remodeling? What would it take to get Maria to see that he was right about that, too?

Another piece of my Miguel...gone. Soon there will be nothing left.

She would never trust him to make those changes. Javy kicked a cracked piece of tile, chipping away at the broken remnant clinging to the floor. She would never trust him with his father's legacy.

He couldn't blame her for her lack of faith. After his father's death, he'd had a load of responsibility dropped on him, and he'd buckled beneath the weight. Once the business had been up and running again, and his mother capable of taking on her old duties, Javy had gladly handed back the reins. In a way, he had been running from responsibility ever since and had been perfectly content to do so.

But watching Emily face her fears and step out on her own made Javy take a close look at his own life, and he was surprised to realize he wasn't entirely happy with what he saw. A few weeks ago, he would have sworn he liked his life exactly as it was—he had his freedom, he could come and go as he pleased and he was responsible only for himself.

You're selfish, Javier. Selfish and irresponsible... You've never stuck with anything in your whole life.

Javy supposed he shouldn't be surprised this latest disaster would bring up old memories of the fight he'd had with his father. Except the memories didn't *feel* old, and the words rang through his thoughts as clearly as the piped-in music that played in the dining room day after day....

The slam of a car door outside broke through Javy's thoughts, and he turned, his heartbeat picking up in anticipation of seeing Emily again. But when the door swung open, his cousin Anna stepped inside.

"Javy." Looking flustered, his typically composed cousin rushed toward him, her purse dangling unevenly against her shoulder, her sunglasses perched on her head and a fistful of papers in one hand. "I'm so sorry. I'm not going to be able to show your friend around this evening."

"Anna—"

"I know, I know. But a potential buyer just called for that monster house in Scottsdale, and it would be a miracle if I got this sale. Your friend will understand, right? I mean, it's not like she was going to make an offer tonight? I've printed off some listings, so the two of you can still take a look. A few of them are having open houses, so you'll be able to see inside. If she likes any of them, call me, and I promise I will meet with her."

She thrust the listings into his hands and spun in a whirlwind of dark hair. He had to jump back to avoid taking a shot below the belt from her purse. Turning back at the last second, she dug into the purse, which could pass for a lethal weapon, and pulled out a handful of colored paper stock. "Here. Take a look at these paint samples for the restaurant, and let me know what you think."

She tossed her last words over her shoulder as she raced from the restaurant, leaving Javy to call after her, "I hate them! And I'm not real thrilled with you right now, either!"

The carved wooden door had swung shut before his last word, and Javy doubted Anna had heard any of his parting shot. Tossing the blindingly bright color samples aside, he glanced at the listings she'd left and then slapped the papers against his thigh with a disgruntled sigh. "Anna…"

Although he supposed he couldn't blame his cousin entirely for this one. Unfortunately, he would be the one to have to break it to Emily that they wouldn't be house hunting that evening. And he really hated disappointing her.

At least if he called her, he could tell her not to waste the trip… But thinking of the sadness her perfect smile failed to hide, he knew she'd been let down enough recently. By her fiancé, by her parents, even by Connor, although admitting that made Javy feel guilty. After all, *his* family had benefited from Connor's actions.

He didn't want her counting him among the people who'd let her down. He'd made her a promise, possibly the first one he'd made to a woman in ten years, and this promise he intended to keep.

Emily pulled up to the restaurant, feeling unaccountably nervous. She'd already met Javy's mother, and Maria Delgado had made no secret about being summarily unimpressed. There was a chance his cousin Anna would react the same.

But, if Emily were completely honest, she couldn't blame all her ping-ponging nerves on the upcoming meeting with Anna or even on the thought of looking for her own place.

In a few minutes, she'd be seeing Javy again. Would he take one look and see how his last words had affected her? That she'd tossed and turned most of the night, imagining how she could thank him in person?

She'd never considered herself particularly inventive, but it was as if Javy's suggestion had cast a spell on her. Their kiss had spun through her thoughts, at first like a tape playing on a loop, but before long, her imagination had taken over where her memory had left off, and she'd pictured his kisses trailing down her throat, drawn to skin left bare by the neckline of her dress, following as it arrowed downward…

Shivers raced along her spine, and her steps slowed as she neared the front door. She felt all too vulnerable to Javier

Delgado's effect on her, one no other man had ever had. With his experience with women, he would certainly know that, but was he affected by the chemistry between them? Or was this all pleasure as usual for him and nothing special at all?

It didn't matter, Emily insisted as she ignored the insignificant twinge in her heart. This was about taking charge for the first time in her life. That was all that mattered. And Javy had arranged for her to meet his cousin, the first step in moving out of her parents' house, which was something Emily definitely wanted.

She shook off her hesitation and opened the door. Her determined strides faltered slightly as she caught sight of Javy on the other side of the empty restaurant, frowning at some papers in his hand. Just the sight of him took her breath away, and Emily used the stolen moment to look at him without those dark eyes looking back and knowing just what she was thinking.

He'd combed his dark hair back from his tanned forehead, taming some of the natural wave, but she could already tell the effort would be temporary at best. Late afternoon light from a nearby window played across his sculpted cheekbones, strong jaw and sensual mouth. Her skin still tingled in every place he'd kissed, a seductive brand that marked her as his…

Emily swallowed and rubbed her palm against a leg of her slacks, as if she could wipe away the memory. She didn't dare allow Javy's kiss, his touch or anything about him have that kind of permanence. Everything about their relationship was temporary—a henna tattoo, not a mark that would scar her for life.

But even with that reminder, proof that Javy was more than fun and games surrounded him. Even in the main dining area, Emily saw the work he'd already accomplished— baseboards torn away from the walls, sections of drywall stripped away to bare studs and wires.

She could only imagine that the bathrooms and hall showed even greater progress. She was amazed by all he'd done, and although she knew he must have had help earlier, at the moment no one else was around.

Including his cousin Anna.

Was there a change in plans? Emily wondered. Had he been so busy that he forgot to call and tell her?

He has a lot on his mind, she argued, with the disappointment dragging down her excitement. *It's completely understandable.*

But understandable or not, it didn't make it any easier to accept that she'd spent almost every moment since they last spoke thinking of him, while she'd completely slipped his mind.

Javy looked up suddenly, stealing her chance to sneak away unnoticed. "Hey," he said, an easy smile replacing his frown. "I have some bad news." He lifted the papers in his hand. "Anna dropped these listings off but had to go meet a client. She's not gonna be able to show you around tonight."

Relief washed over her. "Oh. I thought maybe…" Her voice trailed away as Javy stepped closer.

"Maybe what, Emily?"

"I thought maybe I was early," she said, unwilling to reveal her earlier insecurity.

"Nope, you're right on time. And I'm sorry about Anna."

"You said she left the listings, though, right?"

Javy made a face. "She did, but she printed them off before I could tell her the kind of house you were looking for."

"Well, how could you? I don't know even know what I'm looking for."

"Yeah, I know, but—" he lifted the listings "—you're not looking for these."

Emily's eyebrows rose at the certainty in his voice. "You sound awfully sure of that. Are the houses condemned or something?"

"Of course not. It's just…" Javy sighed. "Last night, I told her that a friend was looking for a house."

"Okay," Emily said slowly, even as she wondered if he kissed all his *friends* the way he'd kissed her.

"She assumed I was talking about a female friend."

"Probably not a big stretch on her part."

"Not exactly," he admitted with an unrepentant smile. "But the thing is, I didn't tell her you were…" His voice trailed away, and he didn't finish his thought.

"What, Javy? What am I?" She could see the debate going on behind his dark eyes.

Finally, on a deep exhale, he said, "Rich. I didn't tell her you were rich."

Emily recoiled at the word. "And that makes a difference?" she asked, only to wonder if she was being foolishly naive once again. It had certainly mattered to Todd. Even with his own family's considerable wealth, he'd needed the Wilson fortune and status to try to get back in his family's good graces.

"No," Javy insisted. "It doesn't make a difference. Not to me."

He stepped closer, invading her space, her senses, her skin… It took everything inside her not to step back and reclaim her own space. But she wasn't sure her shaking knees would support any sudden movement, so she stayed right where she was—caught in the spell of Javy's dark eyes and undeniable masculinity.

"I'm not your fiancé."

Lost in his spell, Emily took a moment to register his words and longer still to try to form a response. "I know that," she insisted, even though Todd's memory had made an unwelcome appearance as soon as Javy mentioned her family's money.

"Do you?" Javy asked, pressing. "I *did* take money from your family. Although I promise you, I didn't know where Connor got the money until recently."

Reaching out, she grasped his arm. "I believe you, Javy."

He was silent so long, Emily feared he didn't believe her, but then the tension thrumming beneath his warm skin caught her attention. Her pulse began to race, until it matched the raw, rhythmic beat she felt in his veins. And every question she had about the strength of his attraction was answered.

The desire dancing beneath his skin might not be anything new, but at least he felt it. At least she wasn't alone in her desperation for another kiss, another touch... But wanting to make sure the matter of her family's money was behind them once and for all, Emily huskily murmured, "What happened back then...none of it was your fault."

His mouth twisting into a wry smile, he warned, "Don't be too sure about that." Without giving Emily the chance to ask what he meant, he said, "Anyway, all I was trying to say is that I didn't give Anna the price range of houses you'd be looking for. She assumed that you'd be looking in more... modest neighborhoods. I recognize some of these addresses, and they're nowhere near where you grew up."

The idea of moving out had hit so suddenly, Emily hadn't had time to give much thought to where she wanted to live. But the idea of a gated golf course community in Scottsdale, where her parents and her sister, Aileen, lived seemed ridiculous. What would she do with six bedrooms and seven thousand square feet, anyway?

"Well, it's not like I'm looking for a mansion. Just a house." A place she could call her own. "This is my decision, and I don't expect my parents to foot the bill." Curiosity lifted Javy's eyebrows, but after her overreaction, Emily realized he wasn't going to ask. "I came into an inheritance from my grandmother when I turned twenty-five. I left most of the money invested in stocks and bonds, but I used some of it to back a friend's boutique. She makes gorgeous fashion jewelry and accessories. She designed the purse I carried at the reception.

"Anyway, I'll be the first to admit I invested in the shop as a way to help a friend rather than expecting some big return, but a few years ago, this movie star fell in love with some of Cassie's pieces, and she was photographed wearing some of the jewelry. From there, everything took off for Cassie. She's opened a second shop in Tempe, and other boutiques are now carrying her designs. It's been amazing."

"Thanks to you."

A glimmer of pride shone in his dark eyes—one Emily instantly tried to suppress. "Oh, no! It was all Cassie. I usually put in a few days during the week at her stores, but only to help out and see her latest designs." She'd taken time off for the wedding and what would have been her honeymoon, but the rest of Cassie's employees could easily cover for her. "I had nothing to do with it."

"You had faith in a friend. You were kind and generous, and you invested in her dream. I seriously doubt Cassie would say that was nothing. She's lucky to have you."

Warmth spread through Emily at his words. She'd never thought of it that way, even though her friend had always given her credit for the part she played as half owner. She only wished she could find a way to convince Javy to believe in *his* dream.

But he'd already refused her money, and despite his praise, Emily honestly wasn't sure she had anything else to offer.

As Javy drove to the first house, Emily poured over the listings his cousin had printed out. She bit her lower lip in focused concentration, which he might have found as amusing as he did arousing if he wasn't worried she was setting herself up for disappointment.

Stopping at a red light, he reached over and brushed a

loose curl behind her ear. Her startled gaze flew to his. "Emily, I'm not sure how to say this, but I don't want you getting your hopes up."

Her turquoise eyes widened. Her lips parted, but no sound emerged. "I'm not," she insisted after that brief pause. "I won't. Really. I don't expect…anything."

"Good, and it's not like you have to make your mind up tonight."

Emily blinked at him. "Okay."

"Anna's a great agent, and she'll take you out to look at as many houses as you want."

Emily breathed a soft laugh and shook her head. "Right. Anna. Houses."

"What?" Javy had to face forward again as the light turned green.

"Nothing. I thought… Never mind what I thought. You're right, though. I don't have to make any decisions tonight."

"I know this is a big deal for you, and I just want you to be happy."

From the corner of his eye, he caught sight of Emily's smile—a little wry, but genuine all the same. "Believe me, I'm working on it."

Her enigmatic response stayed with Javy as he drove her from house to house. He knew finding her own place was one of the things Emily had decided would make her happy. But what else did she have in mind? And how did he fit in with her plans? He liked the idea of making Emily Wilson happy, but he wondered if he wasn't too much like the places on Anna's list.

"It's nice," Emily said, cocking her head as she looked at what could only generously be called a fixer-upper. "But I don't think it's quite me."

No. By no means would he consider the boxy, forty-year-old ranch the embodiment of Emily Wilson. So far, none of the houses fit Emily's style, class or seven-figure price range.

And while he'd meant every word he'd said about her family's wealth not mattering to him, he knew the differences between their lives would make any kind of lasting relationship impossible.

Which was just as well, he insisted. Especially since he'd never done lasting and could barely call his frequent forays into the shallow end of the dating pool relationships.

But that didn't mean he wouldn't do what he could to make Emily happy now, until she realized she belonged in a much more affluent zip code.

"Ready to call it a night?" he asked as he pulled away from the house, leaving the overgrown lawn, sagging roof and listing for-sale sign in the rearview mirror.

"But we haven't seen all the houses yet," Emily protested, poring over the list.

"Is this what you were like in high school?" he asked, glancing at her from the corner of his eye. "Always following the teacher's instructions to the letter?"

"Well, yes," she said, only to temper her defensive response with a laugh. "Pretty pathetic. Always worried about what other people think, right?"

He'd said pretty much the same thing when he'd challenged her on the dance floor the night of Connor and Kelsey's wedding. Now that he knew Emily better, he wished he hadn't. "No, Emily, it's not pathetic. You wanted to give your parents a reason to be proud of you, and you have. Plenty of reasons, actually."

Which was more than he could say.

He could still see the disappointment in his father's expression when he made the announcement that he wouldn't be going to college. At eighteen, he'd felt like he'd spent years chained to a desk. He'd wanted to start his own life—a life that included marriage to the woman he loved.

He and Stephanie had had it all planned. She had a friend in California, on the verge of making it big in movies, who was sure she could get both of them jobs—Stephanie doing walk-on parts and commercials, and Javy working on set designs and behind the scenes.

He'd dropped that bombshell on his parents the night of his graduation, the same night he'd proposed with the simulated ring, which was the best he could afford. He'd gone in expecting a fight, and his father had certainly given him one. He could still remember, almost word for word, how the argument had spun out of control, starting with his father's expected remarks that he and Stephanie were too young, too inexperienced, and building from there, until Javy had felt blindsided by the verbal shots.

You're selfish and irresponsible. How can you even think you'd be a good husband when you've never stuck with anything in your whole life?

He'd vehemently denied every accusation, but within weeks his father's words had been proven true. Once his father got sick, Javy's promises to Stephanie, along with his own dreams of love and marriage, fell to the wayside. He'd been unable to leave his family to pursue the plans they'd made, and he'd learned the hard way that Stephanie wasn't willing to wait. Already in a Hollywood state of mind, she quickly found a stand-in to take his place, all without missing a beat.

And then, as if that hadn't been enough, the fire at the restaurant on *his* watch had burned his father's disappointment into his soul.

Changing the subject, he said, "Why don't we get something to eat and save the rest of the list for another time?"

"One more," she pleaded. "This one is having an open house, so we can see inside."

Maybe the brief trip to the past had more of an effect than he'd expected, but for one surreal moment Emily's words took on a new meaning as her casual use of the word *we* turned into something…not casual as the idea of the two of them looking for a place together swirled through his thoughts.

He gave a mental shake, clearing the idea from his head. Emily hadn't meant anything by that simple two-letter word. He had no reason for alarm, Javy determined, ready to take a calming breath, only to realize he wasn't experiencing any of his typical panicked reactions. No sweaty palms, no choking sensation, no urge to jump from the speeding car just to escape.

"I know this neighborhood," Emily announced suddenly, distracting Javy, who was starting to freak out over how un-freaked out he was. "Kelsey's condo isn't far from here."

Emily leaned forward, straining against the seat belt, her excitement brimming as she looked around at the small, well-kept houses, the flower-lined lawns and the driveways crowned by basketball hoops. Javy followed the street numbers until they came to a row of townhomes.

"Oh, look! They're so cute!" she cried.

She had her seat belt off and was out the door almost before Javy brought the car to a stop in front of a two-story unit marked with an open house sign and a bouquet of colorful balloons. Pale yellow shingle siding topped the redbrick lower level, and yellow-and-white-striped awnings shaded the front windows.

"It's like…like a gingerbread house!" she exclaimed.

"That's about the size of it," Javy said beneath his breath as he circled the car to join Emily on the sidewalk.

Even from the outside, and without glancing at the listing, still clutched in Emily's hand, he could tell the place was tiny. But when Emily turned to him with her blue eyes sparkling and her gorgeous features more animated than he'd seen, any thoughts—negative or otherwise—disappeared.

"I love it," she said, wrapping her arms around her waist, as if trying to contain her excitement.

Javy tossed aside any words of caution. He was here to support Emily on her quest for happiness, not to discourage her dreams. Either she would figure out for herself that the place was way too small or she would turn around and sell it in a year or two, when she started to miss the high-class amenities she could easily afford.

He knew he'd made the right decision when Emily offered him a soul-stealing smile. Her expression turned more seductive than he'd ever seen, though a hint of shyness remained. "I think," she began, only to stop and run her tongue over her bottom lip, "this is the part where I get to thank you in person."

Any protest Javy might have made dried up in his suddenly arid throat as Emily stepped closer. A part of him *wanted* to take credit. Not for showing her the house, but for the spark of feminine confidence in her eyes. He wanted to believe he touched something inside her no other man could. And even though he knew better, he was going to let himself revel in the foolish, potentially dangerous thought…just for a little while.

His pulse pounded in anticipation. Every heartbeat urged him to pull her into his arms and claim her lips with his own, but Emily had accepted the challenge he'd issued, and this was her move.

The control needed in the seconds leading up to the kiss was nothing compared to the tension building inside him as Emily slid a hand around his neck and pulled his head down to hers.

The excitement and anticipation she'd shown at her first glimpse of the town house bubbled up inside her kiss and burst against his tongue. He'd never been one for champagne, never understood the popularity or the price, but he thought maybe the most expensive vintage would taste like Emily, and he suddenly understood paying a thousand dollars a pop.

A brief thought about an addiction to the finer things in life crossed his mind, but he shoved it and every other thought aside to focus on nothing but the feel of Emily in his arms.

Her shirt had inched up ever so slightly, just enough for him to feel her skin against his palms. He trailed his fingers from her smooth back to the curve of her waist and the faint indentation of her hips. He brushed his thumbs against the underside of her rib cage and absorbed the shudder that quaked through her entire body until he felt like *he* was the one shaking.

She whispered his name against his lips as he drew in a much-needed breath, but the split-second window was all reality needed to sneak back in. Somewhere in the complex, a dog barked. A mother called her kids in for dinner, and the scent of barbecue drifted on a hot, dry breeze. Emily blinked up at him, as if waking from the sensual dream holding them captive, to find herself in the middle of a family-friendly neighborhood.

She ducked her head to hide behind her blond hair and offered a half apology, half explanation. "I—I'm sorry. I didn't mean to get, um, carried away. I was just so excited about the house…"

"The house? Really? I thought maybe I had at least something to do with it."

Color burned brighter in her cheeks, and he knew she wasn't ready for him to joke about the undeniable chemistry between them. And considering the number her fiancé had done on her, who could blame her?

But he'd needed to lighten the mood, Javy realized, falling back on old habits to hide how deeply the kiss—and the woman—had affected him. Beating back the uneasy thought that the chemistry between them might be something more than fun and flirtation, he took a deep breath and tried to slow his raging pulse.

Holding out his hand, he said, "Let's go see this house of yours."

Chapter Six

"I can't believe I'm buying a house!" Emily had to raise her voice to be heard above the music and crazed fans watching the basketball play-offs in the crowded bar. When Javy had said he wanted to find someplace to eat, she hadn't expected him to pick a sports bar, but the loud, boisterous atmosphere perfectly fit the emotions bouncing through her.

Javy smiled at her from across the small high-top table. Leaning closer, he said, "Don't get too far ahead of yourself. You still need to have the place inspected before you make an offer."

Don't get too far ahead of yourself....

The warning served a double purpose as she stared into his espresso eyes. Judging by the way she'd completely lost her head when she'd kissed him earlier, it would be all too easy to end up head over heels. And she could end up losing so much more than the house she had her heart set on. If she didn't watch herself around Javy, she could end up losing her heart.

Forcing her focus back onto the town house, she said, "I know, but you've already said the house was in good shape."

"From what I could see, yeah. But you need to let the professionals take a look."

Emily would trust what Javy had to say over some hired professional any day. Which showed she was already in too deep. She'd made the mistake of trusting Todd. Shouldn't she have learned some kind of lesson from her broken engagement?

And yet Javy was so different from Todd, so different from anyone she knew. Todd had cared only about what he wanted, and her parents had focused too much on what they wanted for her.

Javy was the first person who had ever asked her what *she* wanted, and more than that, he actually listened. Which wasn't to say he didn't have his doubts.

"Go ahead," she told him with a wry smile. "You've kept quiet long enough. Let it all out. You think I'm rushing this, and you're trying to find a way to tell me without hurting my feelings."

"Well, I'm glad you've picked up on what a sensitive guy I am," he said with his usual grin before he shook his head, "but, nah, I'm not gonna say it."

"Why not? I know it's what you're thinking."

"Maybe," he confessed. "But I'm also thinking you're a grown woman who knows her own mind. I watched your face light up when you saw that house. Something tells me you haven't been so excited about something for a long time." Leaning forward, his fingers traced from her forehead to her ear as he brushed a locked of hair away from her face. "It's a bit of a challenge, you know?"

Eyes widening, she asked, "What is?"

"Trying to figure out what I can do to make you light up like that when you see me."

Feeling her face heat up, Emily bet she was putting the neon beer signs to shame. "I don't think I'm much of a challenge."

She was a novice and Javy was the expert when it came to flirting, dating, making love... She didn't stand a chance, and if she were smart, she'd run in the opposite direction. But she sat frozen, caught in the spell he wove with his voice, his touch, the slumberous burn in his dark eyes. When Emily finally found the strength to move, she didn't pull away. Instead, she leaned forward, melting into the heat of his hand.

"Javy..." Her stuck-in-the-throat whisper was barely audible over the cheers of the crowd and the loud music, but Emily heard another female voice, clear as day, calling out his name.

Startled, she turned in time to see a gorgeous brunette weaving her way in time with the music through tables and chairs and groups of people to reach Javy's side. The woman turned more than a few heads as she brushed by several guys, most of whom did double takes at her thick mane of chestnut hair, wide smile and feminine curves, readily displayed by a lollipop-red tank top and denim skirt.

"Monica!" Javy rose and greeted the woman with a smile and a kiss on the cheek. "It's good to see you! How long has it been?"

"Has to be six months, right? Your family's Christmas party," said the woman.

"Was that the last time?" He shook his head, a look of nostalgia, and...something else, which Emily couldn't identify, crossing his features.

What was it? she wondered. Sorrow over the way things had ended? Sympathy for leaving another broken heart in his wake? She didn't know Javy well enough to read the subtleties of his expression, but she did know his reputation.

"I heard about the restaurant." Concern shone in the woman's eyes. "How long do you think you'll be shut down?"

"Not long. As soon as the damage is repaired, we'll be up and running again," Javy replied.

"I bet Maria's glad about that," Monica said, the warmth in her voice taking Emily by surprise.

Emily knew she had a strike against her as far as Maria was concerned, thanks to her past with Connor. She also assumed Javy's mother didn't believe any woman was good enough for her son, so she tried not to take Maria's criticism personally. But Monica's obvious affection for the older woman spoke of a close enough relationship to make Emily reconsider.

"Speaking of my mother, it's a good thing she's not here, or she'd be smacking me for forgetting my manners," said Javy. "Monica, I'd like you to meet Emily Wilson. Emily, this is Monica Carter, an old friend."

Emily wasn't exactly sure of proper etiquette when introduced to an ex-girlfriend while on a date—if this was a date—but Monica merely smiled and held out her hand. "Hi. Nice to meet you," she said, without showing the least bit of reaction at being introduced as an "old friend."

But then again, hadn't Javy used that same term when he'd told his cousin about *her?* Which, Emily supposed, answered her unasked question from earlier that evening. Maybe Javy *did* kiss all his friends the way he kissed her.

"It's…nice to meet you, too," Emily replied a little weakly to the brunette's easygoing greeting.

Six months down the road, if she ran into Javy with another woman, he'd no doubt refer to her as an old friend, as well. And Emily could only hope she would respond with as much casual and carefree grace as Monica Carter had.

Emily pulled up to the town house the next morning and breathed a sigh of relief. The place was exactly as she remembered and just as charming in daylight as it had been the evening before.

She was meeting Javy's cousin, and Anna had sounded so excited, not only about a possible sale, but about the fact that Emily had liked one of the houses. Her enthusiasm was exactly what Emily needed, since her parents, whom she'd also asked to meet her at the town house, weren't likely to be as thrilled.

"This is what I want," she whispered as she cut the engine and reached for her purse.

She only wished she could be so certain about other aspects of her life.

She'd purposely decided not to ask Javy to come along. Partly because it wouldn't be fair to throw him into what might be an uncomfortable situation, but mostly because she wasn't sure how she felt after running into one of Javy's *friends* the night before.

Even after Monica left, the sensual spell Javy cast had remained broken, and Emily had soon made an excuse to leave. She'd told him she had a lot to think about, but while the possibility of buying a house should have held her complete attention, her mind had drifted more often than not back to Javy.

Aware of his reputation from the start, Emily shouldn't have been surprised to run across one of his former flames. But knowing those women existed and coming face-to-face with a woman as beautiful and confident as Monica were two different things. Emily didn't quite know how to handle the latter.

You're jealous, an all-knowing voice accused. *Jealous of the women in Javy's past and the women in his future.*

Because there *would* be women in Javy's future. If she couldn't come to grips with that now, she needed to let go. Trying to hold on would bring a boatload of heartache.

The sound of an approaching car interrupted her thoughts.

A dark-haired woman sporting a pair of oversize sunglasses waved from behind the wheel of a small, red compact. As she climbed from the car, she pushed her glasses to the top of her head, and Emily could see enough of a resemblance to know this had to be Javy's cousin.

"Emily? Of course you're Emily. I mean, look at you." Before Emily could respond to that statement, the woman held out her hand. "I'm Anna Delgado."

"Nice to meet you."

"You, too. I apologize for not showing you around yesterday. I know you saw this place last night, during the open house, but you can't rob me of giving you the grand tour. It's my favorite part of the job," Anna said as she led the way up the driveway. "After that, we'll get down to my least favorite part, the paperwork."

Emily followed as Anna opened the front door and swept inside.

"I love the way the foyer opens up to the vaulted ceiling and gives the place a larger feel," Anna commented.

Emily nodded as she got her second look at the house she soon planned to call home. The tile foyer led into the great room. Sunlight streamed through the shutters, casting striped shadows over the beige carpet. The ceiling fan whirred overhead, a seasonal contrast to the brick fireplace on the far wall. The mantle held a few pictures, posed portraits and casual snapshots of the current owners, but Emily could already picture her own displays lining the wide oak surface.

As Anna led the way upstairs to the bedrooms, she discussed pricing and the strategy of making a reasonable offer. The ringing of the doorbell interrupted her, and she turned to Emily with a questioning lift to her eyebrows.

"That would be my parents," Emily explained. "I didn't exactly tell them I wanted to make an offer on this house."

"Oh," Anna said knowingly.

Yes, Emily thought, nerves kicking in at the prospect of confronting her parents. *As in uh-oh.*

"You want to buy a house?" Gordon Wilson repeated, doubt written in every line of his furrowed brow.

Emily had anticipated her parents' disapproval and hoped the house might charm them into accepting her decision, but her mother especially appeared anything but charmed as she looked around the dining room, mere steps from the kitchen on one side and the great room on the other.

"This house?" her mother asked. "Emily, if you're interested in investing in a home, why not let us help you to make the right decision?"

Like they'd *helped* decide her friends, her hobbies, her courses at school…even her fiancé. Although, she'd succumbed to Todd's golden-boy looks and high-polished charm before her parents met him, their immediate approval made it too easy for her to ignore the doubts that had started swirling during her short engagement.

If not for Connor, she would have ignored those doubts all the way to the altar. She would have been miserable, not only because she would have been married to an unfaithful liar, but because she'd have married a man against her better judgment simply to make her parents happy.

"This *is* the right place," Emily insisted. "And I found it on my own."

"It's—it's a town house!" Charlene argued. "Did you even look at the master bedroom? Your closet at home is bigger than that entire room."

"I guess I'll be getting rid of some things, then," Emily replied.

Her parents exchanged a look filled with worry and silent

frustration. "Emily, you need to take some time and think this through," her father said, using the calm, reasonable tone that always made her feel like a petulant child and never failed to quell any opposing ideas.

Not this time. Emily repeated the words as if she could talk some steel into her spine.

"Let's go back home and discuss this decision. After all, there's no rush. After a few days, we'll see if you still want to make an offer," her father added.

And after a few days, her father fully expected that she would cave. That their *talks* of how she was making a mistake, how she was rushing into things, and how she was ultimately incapable of knowing her own mind would wear her down until she didn't have a high heel left to stand on.

What do you want?

The familiar whisper spun through her thoughts, but while Javy's husky voice normally left her weak, the answer to the question and the faith he'd showed in her made her strong.

"I want this house," Emily said.

Her father sighed, as if dealing with a two-year-old stomping her feet in a tantrum. "There's more to owning a house than finding one you like. You might like the way this place looks," he said, the doubt in his voice expressing his confusion as to *why* she liked it, "but what about all you can't see? What about the wiring? The foundation? The plumbing?"

Javy immediately came to Emily's mind. He would help or know someone who could. After all, he was the one to introduce her to Anna. He and his cousin Alex were making repairs to the restaurant. Javy was...

"Things might be fine now, but what about two or three months from now?" her father asked, pressing.

...not someone she could rely on.

Everything Emily knew told her that. Oh, sure, right now

he was charming and attentive. When she was with him, he made her feel like she was the only woman in the world, but last night had proved that wasn't true. The world was filled with women like Monica, and before long, Emily would be counted among them—a woman Javy would introduce as an old friend to the next woman he dated.

Her stomach twisted at the thought, but Emily forced herself to face it. Ignoring a problem only made it that much harder deal with—her engagement to Todd had taught her that. If she'd taken a good, hard look at Todd two months ago, she might have seen beyond the surface to the faulty wiring beneath. But she hadn't, and she had the humiliation of a broken engagement to show for it.

And maybe she was making the same mistake again. Rushing in without thinking the decision through. She really didn't need another failure right now. What if she couldn't handle a house of her own? Wouldn't moving back home, admitting she'd been wrong and that her parents had been right, be so much worse than simply staying where she was?

What do you want?

Javy's voice rang through her thoughts, but maybe that question didn't really matter as long as what she wanted was something she couldn't have.

Chapter Seven

"Man, what time did you get started this morning?"

Javy looked away from the tile he'd been ruthlessly tearing up to meet his cousin Alex's gaze. After pushing the safety glasses up to the top of his head, he wiped his forehead with the sweatband he wore on one wrist. "'Bout an hour ago," he said.

His cousin let out a low whistle. "And you got all this done?" Alex asked as he looked at the broken remains of a large section of the dining-room tile.

The two of them had worked together the day before on tearing out the tile in the bathrooms and hallway, saving the largest area for last.

"I was feeling motivated," Javy said.

When Anna had called yesterday to tell him she was meeting Emily at the house, he'd been happy for Emily. He'd been less than happy as the hours passed and Anna's call was the only one he received. He had fully expected to hear from Emily and didn't quite know what to think of her not calling.

And, yeah, okay, he could have picked up the phone, too, but *Emily* was the one with the big news. It only made sense that she would want to call him.

So he'd gone to bed, secure in his decision *not* to call Emily, only to spend a few restless hours wondering why she hadn't called. He'd finally reached for the phone, determined to find out, but then he'd noticed it was one o'clock in the morning and he was certifiably insane.

He'd never, *never* lost a moment's sleep over a woman not calling. He knew he had a reputation as a ladies' man, but he also knew every woman was different. Each had her own taste and opinion, and if one woman wasn't interested, more than likely another woman was.

Those same rules applied to Emily. If she wasn't interested…except, dammit, she *was* interested! He knew she was.

Giving in to frustration, he picked up his hammer and chisel and took another whack at the tile.

"Hey, *primo,* safety glasses, remember?" said Alex. "You won't be so irresistible to the girls wearing a patch over one eye!"

Javy swore beneath his breath, knowing his cousin was right, and lowered the glasses before picking up the hammer again.

"You know, we just might get this done today," Alex said over Javy's relentless pounding. Judging the remaining area with a critical eye, he added, "If we finish the other repairs and patch the floors tomorrow, we can get the new tile laid in the next few days. I'd say you can start planning for a reopening next weekend."

Javy sank back on his haunches. His calves and ankles were already groaning a protest after the hours he'd spent crouching on his knees. If Alex's time frame held true, Javy wasn't going to have much of a chance to sand and refinish his father's damaged furniture before the reopening.

Of course, all the time in the world wouldn't make a difference if he couldn't do the job. Still, he owed it to his father to try, to prove in some way that he was no longer the selfish, irresponsible boy his father had seen all those years ago. That he was more than the selfish, irresponsible man he'd become.

He thought of the confidence and encouragement in Emily's eyes. He owed it to *himself* to try.

"Think you could help me haul some of the damaged dining-room furniture back to my place? It's in the way here, and my mother doesn't think the worst of the pieces are worth saving."

If Alex thought Javy's house was a strange place to take the furniture, he didn't let it show. Instead, he merely said, "Yeah, sure. I'll hook up the trailer, and we'll be able to get it all in one trip."

"Thanks, man. And thanks for all the work you've done here."

"Hey, it's the least I can do."

Alex's words rang in Javy's mind even as his cousin picked up his own hammer, slid on a pair of safety glasses and started to work. Recently Javy had felt like everything in his life was the least he could do. The *very* least. Yeah, he put in the hours and the effort at the restaurant; he showed up for all the family get-togethers; he made sure to catch a game with the guys or hit the basketball court for some one-on-one every other week or so.

But when was the last time he'd looked forward to any of it? He gave a short laugh. He'd felt more satisfaction in the last few days, trying to get the restaurant reopened, than he had when the place was running smoothly. And how messed up was it that he needed a disaster to give his life meaning?

"You say something?" Alex asked, ceasing the relentless hammering for a moment.

"No, I was just… I've been thinking of talking to my mother about my ideas for the bar and patio again. Now would be the perfect chance. We're already closed, and if we keep on your schedule, the repairs will be done sooner than we thought. Why not move on to the renovations?"

"If Maria says yes, I'll have a crew ready to start the next day," his cousin said, even as he raised a doubting eyebrow.

"But you don't think she will?"

Alex shrugged. "She was pretty adamant about not changing a thing. And can you blame her? If it ain't broke, don't fix it," he said, a familiar stubbornness underscoring his words. One that had nothing to do with Maria's perspective or the restaurant.

"Yeah, well, speaking of things you broke by *not* fixing them," Javy scoffed, "I saw Monica the other night."

He'd waited until his cousin was taking a swing to make that comment, and Alex's well-aimed hammer clanked off the side of the chisel before bouncing off the tile. "Where? Why didn't you tell me before?"

Javy shrugged, taking his time and executing a few solid hits before answering. "You *did* break up with her, right? Because she wanted a commitment, and you wanted your freedom."

"That's right," Alex said with an arrogance that could only come from being completely wrong and knowing it.

"So, what difference would it make if Monica found someone who's serious about her?"

"Has she?" Alex jumped to his feet, hammer clutched in his hand, as if his competition was going to come busting through the door any minute. "Was she out with some other guy?"

With Emily Wilson seated across from him, Javy wouldn't have noticed if Monica was out with the entire Arizona Cardinals defensive line. But as distracted as he'd been, he wasn't completely blind. Monica was a beautiful woman. It wouldn't have surprised anyone—except maybe Alex—if she'd found someone else.

"No, but why would you care? You've got your freedom, man."

"Yeah, right," Alex muttered before sinking back down on his knee pads and attacking the tile with a vengeance.

Javy shook his head. What was it with the people in his family? So stubborn, so averse to any kind of change.

And what about you? a subversive voice whispered. *What would it take to make you settle down?*

Emily's face flashed before his eyes, despite his attempts to push thoughts of her aside.

Emily's not looking for a relationship, he mentally insisted.

After calling off her engagement days before the wedding, he was sure she wasn't looking for anything other than a good time. And maybe to reaffirm that she was a beautiful, desirable woman, despite her fiancé's infidelity. She was *not* looking for anything permanent.

And if that changed? If Emily started wanting more?

Would he fall back into old habits? Or would he be willing to embrace something new?

Later that afternoon Anna breezed into the restaurant, pushing her sunglasses to the top of her head to look around. "Wow!" she exclaimed. "I can't believe you've done so much since yesterday. Did you have a chance to look at the paint samples I left?"

Javy rolled his eyes toward Alex. Earlier the two of them had agreed they wouldn't want to paint the restaurant—or anything else, for that matter—any color Anna had chosen.

"We're going out on a limb this time and painting the walls exactly the colors they already are," Alex said.

Anna huffed a sigh. "Honestly, the two of you are pathetically afraid of change."

Alex voiced an immediate protest, but Anna's words mirrored Javy's earlier thoughts too closely for him to offer a defense. Instead, he asked Anna, "So what's going on? Or did you just stop by to check up on us?"

Javy expected some kind of comeback and was surprised when his cousin frowned. "Actually, I need to talk to you, if you've got a minute."

"Yeah, I guess I could take a break," Javy told her.

"He needs one. He's been at this since dawn. If I didn't know better—" Alex laughed "—I'd think he had woman troubles. But we know that can't be it. The only trouble Javy's ever had with women is not having enough hours in the day to date them all."

Javy frowned. It was an old joke, one he'd made himself. Yet, somehow, hearing it now sounded…wrong. Especially when Emily's face flashed through his mind.

Leading the way into the kitchen, he grabbed a water from the stainless-steel fridge. After downing half the bottle in one swallow, he asked Anna, "What's up?"

"It's about your friend Emily," she began.

"Did she make an offer on the town house?" he asked, purposely keeping his voice casual. Annoyed he had to ask a question he should already know the answer to.

"No."

That answer wasn't the one he'd expected to hear, not from Anna or from Emily. "What the hell happened?" He set the plastic bottle down on the stainless-steel countertop with a watery thunk. "She was ready to pull out her checkbook the minute we saw the place!"

"She seemed pretty excited until her parents showed up. They really did a number on her, telling her she was rushing the decision and not thinking things through. She said she wanted to take a few days to think it over, but I've heard from the agent representing the seller. She's showing the house to a couple this afternoon. I don't want to push, but I'd hate for Emily to miss out if she really wants this house."

"Emily wants it." He had seen the excitement shining in her turquoise eyes and knew she had her heart set on the small town house. A slow anger started burning inside him when he thought of her parents crushing that desire. "Let me talk to her and—"

"Are you sure that's a good idea?" Anna asked, her forehead creasing in a worried frown.

"She needs to know someone else is looking at the house. I'm surprised you haven't called already."

"I promised her a few days to think about it," Anna said defensively. "Besides, what I meant was, are you sure it's a good idea for *you* to call her?"

"What's that supposed to mean?"

"You've done this whole 'rescue the damsel in distress' thing before, Javy," his cousin said softly. "I don't want to see you get hurt again."

Javy tensed at the reminder of his past. "You are not comparing Emily to Stephanie," he said, his voice flat with denial.

Thanks to ten years' worth of wisdom and hindsight, Javy now knew that his ex-girlfriend had likely suffered from depression. From moment to moment, she had alternated between anger over the past, despair over the present and impossibly high hopes for the future—their future.

After her troubled home life, Javy couldn't blame her for her desperation to escape. Stephanie's parents had spent her childhood in and out of court, fighting each other and fighting over her. And he had promised her he would take her away from all that, promised her they would have a life together. In return, she'd sworn she would wait.

In the end, Javy supposed neither of them had kept their word.

But that decade-old history had nothing to do with here and now. Nothing to do with Emily.

"So you don't think Emily is trying to escape her parents' control by buying a house?" Anna asked.

"Even if she is," he said, "she doesn't need me for that."

Emily didn't need him, period. And that was fine. He'd made a habit of not needing or being needed by anyone. He'd learned that lesson the day Stephanie had ran off with another guy, one who could give her all Javy had promised and more.

"Oh, really?" Anna challenged. "Then why were you going to call her?"

His mind went completely blank. He was unable to explain—or deny—his urge to call Emily. Fortunately, Anna's phone rang before he had a chance to respond…or admit he had nothing to say in his defense.

His cousin immediately flipped her phone open. "Hello? Oh, I see. Yes, I'll let my client know."

She talked for a moment more before disconnecting the call and taking her sweet time putting her cell away. "That was the seller's agent." Disappointment filled Anna's expression. "The couple has made an offer."

When Emily had promised her parents she would take a day or two to think about the town house before making a final decision, she hadn't realized how those days would crawl by.

Sitting in the living room, she flipped through a magazine, which couldn't keep her attention from wandering. If she didn't take this chance now, where would she be one, two, ten years from now? Emily had the sinking feeling she'd still be where she was right then, living with her parents and watching her life tick by.

When the doorbell rang, Emily jumped to her feet, the magazine falling to the floor. She scooped it up and tossed it onto the couch before rushing down the hall. She'd welcome any excuse to break the monotony, but as she neared the carved wooden door, Javy's face flashed in front of her eyes. Which was crazy. He hadn't even called; there was no reason to think he'd suddenly show up at the house.

But when she turned the door handle, her heart refused to listen to her head. Her heartbeat quickening in anticipation, she met the gaze of a young woman in a delivery uniform. Thinking the disappointment her due for setting her hopes far too high, Emily signed for the package and closed the door. She glanced at the return address and felt her stomach sink even further.

As part of the wedding reception, Kelsey had taken old photos of Emily and Todd to an audiovisual specialist to create a program meant to play throughout the night. Kelsey's friend had promised to return the photos, and that must be what was inside the envelope printed with the words "Do Not Bend."

Forget bending—she would have liked to burn the whole thing, but she might as well return her childhood photos to the albums her parents kept in the study. She'd decide later what to do with the few pictures Todd had provided.

After tossing those aside, Emily arranged her own photos in chronological order. As she slid stolen moments of her life back into place, she recalled when the photographs were taken. A dinner party at the governor's mansion. A family ski trip. A ballet recital. She remembered the events, but looking at the photos was like seeing paper-doll versions of herself, each new outfit representing a different aspect of her life. Social Life Emily… Sporty Emily… Dancer Emily…

But who was beneath the interchangeable wardrobes? Who was she inside?

She turned over another picture and gave a surprised laugh. "Aileen," she murmured. Undoubtedly, her sister had slipped the photo of Emily as a naked, diaper-waving toddler into the bunch.

"Well, there we have it. My true calling. I'm meant to be a stripper," Emily said wryly. "My parents will be so proud." She flipped the album page to slide the photo back in place but stopped short when she saw a picture of her aunt Olivia.

Kelsey's mother had left home when Emily was only three. She had no memories of her father's rebellious younger sister, but she'd heard the whispers all her life of how much she looked like her aunt. As she scrutinized Olivia's picture, Emily could certainly see the resemblance in the blond hair, blue eyes and similar features.

But beyond superficial details, Emily couldn't imagine someone more different. Olivia had defied her father, choosing the man she loved over the family fortune. Unfortunately for Olivia, the man she loved hadn't done the same. Donnie Mardell, Kelsey's father, had taken the money Olivia's father offered and had left town. Olivia could have come home, tail tucked between her legs, but she hadn't. Instead, she'd struck out on her own, making a life for herself and Kelsey.

Tracing a finger over her aunt's image, Emily could only think for all their outward similarities, inside…

"We're so different," she whispered. Like the cicadas that shed their skins along the fence that lined her family's property, outwardly the shell looked exactly the same, but inside it was hollow and empty. She felt hollow and empty.

A feeling that would only get worse if she didn't at least try…

After putting away the albums, Emily raced down the hall. Once she reached her bedroom, she pulled her cell phone and Anna's card from her purse. Dialing the number, she waited impatiently for the other woman to answer. Anna barely had the chance to say hello before Emily said, "Anna, it's Emily Wilson."

"Emily! We were just getting ready to call you."

"We?"

"I'm at the restaurant with Javy."

"Oh." Emily fought the temptation to ask to speak with him. Just hearing his voice would go a long way toward bolstering her confidence, but this decision couldn't be about Javy any more than it could be about her parents. Exchanging one crutch for another wouldn't help her to stand on her own. "Well, I'm calling to make an offer on the house."

Emily was expecting an excited response from the other woman, and Anna's hesitation had her hopes dropping to the pit of her stomach. "Emily, someone else has made an offer."

Sinking onto her bed, Emily said, "So, that's it. I've lost my chance."

She'd let her fears and insecurities rob her of her dream. There were other houses, but she would always be left to wonder *what if?* And the similarities between the house and her possible relationship with Javy certainly weren't lost on Emily.

So sure she'd already missed out, Anna's next words didn't immediately register. "No, no, it's not too late. Or at least, it might not be. The seller hasn't accepted the offer yet. Their agent knows you are interested, and I think they're hoping you'll make a better offer."

It was on the tip of Emily's tongue to ask Anna what she should do, but instead she stayed silent. Certainly, she had the means to offer above the seller's asking price, pretty much guaranteeing the house would be hers. But no one needed to tell her that wasn't good business sense.

Taking a deep breath, she said, "I want to make an offer of ten percent less than the asking price, like we originally discussed."

After making plans to meet Anna at the restaurant to finalize the paperwork for the offer, Emily snapped her phone shut and grabbed her purse. Her heart pounding in anticipation, she only hoped she wasn't too late to have the house she wanted…or to have the man she was wanting more and more.

Chapter Eight

Javy knew the instant Emily walked into the restaurant. The noise level of work around him gradually dropped off. Conversations trailed away, the scrape of the shovel against concrete as Tommy scooped up and dumped the broken tile into a trash barrel faded, and finally the pounding of Alex's hammer ceased. For a split second, Javy's ears rang with the silence. After hours of chipping away at the tile, a cacophony reminiscent of dozens of plates shattering over and over again, quiet was a blessed relief.

Glancing over his shoulder, he saw Emily standing amid the chaos and destruction. One look, and he could certainly understand why all work in the restaurant had come to a stop. One look, and it felt like everything had come to a stop inside him: his heart, his breath, his capacity for rational thought.

Alex recovered first, jumping to his feet and pushing the safety glasses to the top of his head. "Morning. The restaurant's closed right now, but we're having a grand re-opening next Saturday if you'd like to come back—"

Emily's gaze shifted to Javy. "It's okay," he said as he slowly stood. "Emily's here to see Anna."

It had been his cousin's idea for Emily to come to the restaurant. Anna had given a long-winded excuse about saving herself a trip, since she wanted to stop by an open house not far away. Javy hadn't bought it at the time, and the story had lost all credibility when Anna suddenly realized she didn't have all the necessary paperwork and had to run back to her office, anyway.

Oh, but no need to call Emily, since she was already on her way.

His cousin was about as subtle as her paint swatches.

"So, where is Anna?" Emily asked, her smile a little too bright, but not enough to blind him from seeing the flicker of hurt in her eyes from the way he'd brushed off her arrival.

Biting back a curse, he explained his cousin's absence. "She'll be back in a few minutes."

Time, Anna clearly thought, he should use to talk to Emily, but for the first time since they'd met, an uncomfortable silence fell between them. He didn't want to consider that Emily could be anything like Stephanie, but the lightning speed of her flip-flopping decisions was reminiscent of his ex. Stephanie had sworn she wanted him and would wait for him—right up to the day she didn't.

"You must be happy with all the progress you've made," Emily said finally. "And you're having the reopening next weekend?"

Gradually becoming aware that work around them had started up again, Javy led her away from the dining room and around the corner to the bar area.

"I'm thinking Saturday night. That'll give us an extra day in case Alex's timetable is off a little."

"You'll get it done," Emily said. The confidence she showed in him was almost as tempting as the attraction he'd felt from the start. But could he really trust any of it?

"You know, I really thought you'd make an offer on the house when you met with Anna yesterday," he said bluntly.

Emily's hands tightened on her purse strap. "I know. And I wanted to. I really did. But it's like I told you the night of Connor and Kelsey's wedding…world's biggest coward."

Disappointment clouded Emily's expression, instantly dousing his distrust. Anna was wrong. So was he for listening to his cousin and letting doubts get the best of him. Emily was nothing like his ex-girlfriend. Yes, she'd suffered a moment's uncertainty, but she hadn't completely changed her mind, hadn't thrown all her plans away the minute she ran into a challenge.

"And like I told *you,*" he reminded her, "I think you're the bravest woman I've ever met."

"And I still think you're wrong."

"But you're making an offer on the house, right?"

"Right."

"So whatever happened yesterday doesn't matter. Today matters, and today you're taking a big step. I'm proud of you."

Emily blinked, and her smile trembled slightly, perfection giving way to genuine emotion. "Thank you. I think that's the nicest thing anyone's ever said to me."

"Now who's being nice? A woman as beautiful as you are must hear compliments every day of her life."

Emily shrugged. "I suppose. But that's just the outside. It doesn't have anything to do with the real me, who I am inside. Even from the start, though, you saw more than that. You see the person I want to be—a woman who *is* brave enough to go after what she wants."

Javy shook his head, uncomfortable with the credit. "That

had nothing to do with me. It's all about you, Emily. All about who you are inside."

"Think so?"

"Know so," he answered, watching her step closer, the confident, sexy spark in her turquoise eyes making her so much more than beautiful on the outside. And if he hadn't been turned on before, there was no question that his pulse started pounding out a salsa beat when she stopped a breath away.

He reached up to urge her closer but stopped when he caught sight of the grimy sweatband on his forearm and the streaks of dirt marking his hand. How could he have forgotten that he'd spent the morning doing backbreaking labor? He'd never been afraid of hard work or of getting dirty, but he took pride in looking his best and doing his best to impress the woman he was interested in. He enjoyed the pursuit and all the trappings that went along with a seduction—flowers, wine, romance....

Nothing about the restaurant, with its haze of dust, dank-smelling air, and symphony of destruction coming from the other room, held even a hint of romance. And neither did he. "I'm a mess," he argued, taking a quick step back.

Emily immediately countered. "I don't care."

"I do," he insisted. He knew she was accustomed to only the best. And while he had enough of an ego to handle dating a woman as beautiful and elegant as Emily, he also had enough class to refrain from touching her when he was dirty, sweaty and...

"I don't care," Emily repeated, her eyes steady on his as she leaned closer.

At the first brush of her lips against his, Javy's hands clenched into fists. Every muscle in his body screamed to reach out, drag Emily into his arms and crush her soft curves against him, but he fought back the urge.

This was her dance and her chance to lead, even if it killed him to be the one to follow. And as she kissed him again and again, he thought it just might.

The only point of contact was still the catch and release of her lips against his, but Emily pulled him deeper and deeper until he wasn't sure what turned him on more—everything her kiss gave…or everything it held back.

The sound of a voice clearing loudly a few feet away broke the moment, which would have gone on forever if Javy had had his way, and he pulled his gaze from Emily's passion-filled eyes and damp lips to meet Anna's smug smile.

"Sorry to interrupt," Anna interrupted, sounding anything but sorry, "but don't start the celebration too early. We still have to make our offer."

"Okay, that's it," Anna said as Emily signed the last page.

They had moved into the restaurant's crowded office. After stacking the pages together, Anna slid them into the fax machine and sent them off with a push of a button.

"Thank you again for your help, and I'm sorry about yesterday," Emily replied. "I truly had planned to make an offer when I met with you at the house but—"

"Hey, no need to apologize. It's a big decision, and I have parents, too, you know. And brothers and sisters. Aunts, uncles, cousins…" Anna let her last word trailed off with an expectant lift to her eyebrows.

When Emily didn't take the bait, Anna leaned against the beat-up desk that housed the fax machine, phone, computer, and a dozen or so photos of the Delgado family. With its warm colors and casual feel, the office blended in perfectly with the rest of the restaurant. But the office had a few masculine hints—an Arizona Cardinals coffee cup, a baseball cap, hung on the inside door handle, and a calendar showcasing muscle cars—telling Emily this was Javy's space.

Emily expected a not-so-subtle interrogation about her relationship with Javy and the kiss Anna had walked in on, but the next comment caught her off guard.

"I didn't mean to eavesdrop when you were talking to your parents the other day, but I heard you say that you'll need to get rid of some things when you move. If you're interested, my mother volunteers for a charity that collects clothes for women trying to get back on their feet after leaving abusive relationships. It's a good cause, and they'd be thrilled with anything you're looking to give away."

"That sounds great. But what if my offer isn't accepted?" Emily hated to think of losing the town house, but she had to face the possibility.

"First, I have a really good feeling about your offer. And second, am I your Realtor, or am I not your Realtor?"

"Um, you're my Realtor?"

"Exactly. And I *will* find you a house," Anna vowed.

Emily smiled at the woman's certainty. And hanging on to a huge closet full of clothes suddenly seemed too much like clinging to the past. It was time to let go, and she had little reason to hold on to dozens of outfits that wouldn't fit in her new house or new life.

"Why don't you have your mother call me?" Emily suggested. "There's no sense in moving a closet full of clothes I won't have room to store."

"Perfect! My mother will be ecstatic."

"At least *one* of our mothers will be," Emily said wryly.

Anna pointed a confident finger Emily's way. "Your parents will come around. Right now they see you as their little girl, someone to protect and take care of. But with the changes you're making, they'll have no choice but to see the new you."

"I hope you're right."

"I am, you'll see. It's like I keep telling Javy. Until he

makes some changes, Maria will still see him as an irresponsible kid."

"Irresponsible!" Emily echoed, indignation for Javy's sake shooting like sparks through her system. "How could she possibly think that?" She waved an arm toward the sound of hard work still going on in the dining area. "After the way he has coordinated the repairs and made sure some of the staff are still able to work right now? That doesn't sound like an irresponsible kid to me."

A small smile tugged at Anna's lips as she listened to Emily's vehement defense. "It's not the way Javy works that's the problem. It's the way he…" She caught herself mid-comment, censoring what Emily knew would have been a remark about the way her cousin played and his carousel of women. "But none of that matters now," Anna added with enough certainty to jump-start a tiny flicker of hope deep inside Emily's chest, one that Emily instantly squashed.

She was not going to set herself up for a fall. She refused to believe in the impossible simply because she wanted it to be true. Javy was all about having fun and enjoying a good time while it lasted, and Emily refused to hope for more.

Like so many of Javy's other women, she was only along for the ride.

Javy didn't think he'd ever take blessed silence or manual labor for granted again. After two full days of pounding, chipping, scraping and hauling away tile, thinset and grout, he didn't think he would ever get the cacophony of sounds out his head. Forget about getting the dust and dirt out of his pores. He'd give just about anything for a hot tub and a cold beer.

A hot tub, a cold beer and Emily would pretty much be a dream come true.

She'd left after signing the offer on the town house, with

the promise to call as soon as she heard anything from his cousin. But long after she'd gone, long after it was possible, the smell of her skin and the sweetness of her kiss tempted him. Despite the dust and grime and sweat, her fresh, clean floral scent stayed with him, and every drink of water he took was flavored with her taste.

"How about calling it a night?" he said to Tommy. The night manager had been at the restaurant since morning, and he was the last of the staff to remain. Even Alex had taken off an hour or so ago, wanting to check on a few of his ongoing jobs before he lost daylight.

"Are you sure?" Tommy wiped at the sweat on his forehead, revealing the only semiclean patch of skin on his entire face.

"Yeah, I'm sure."

True to Alex's word, they had completed the dining-area tear out. All that remained was a final cleanup of shards of broken tile and dust littering the now exposed concrete floors.

"Go on home. I'll finish up," Javy insisted, even though it meant putting his idea of a cold beer on ice for a little longer.

After a quick nod, Tommy split from the restaurant so fast, the kid practically left in a cloud of dust.

"To be nineteen again," Javy murmured, only to realize immediately that he wouldn't want to relive that dark period of his life again for anything.

Not even for the energy of youth, he thought as his muscles groaned in protest as he reached for the push broom leaning against the wall. He wasn't sure how much time had passed before he looked up at a slight sound. Either his ears were still ringing or he was more tired than he thought, but he'd completely missed his mother's arrival through the back door of the restaurant.

He'd known how impossible keeping Maria away would

be. Still, he'd hoped to spare Maria from seeing the place like this. Forcing a positive note into his voice, he said, "Alex and I got a lot done today. He says we'll be ready by this weekend."

Stock-still in the middle of the dining area, his mother looked around. "How?" she asked, disbelief written in her dark eyes.

"I know it looks bad," he said, but as he looked around, all he could see was the hard work everyone had done—Alex, his crew, Tommy and the rest of the staff. "But with even more hard work, we'll get it done, Mama."

"But why tear up the dining room? The broken tile, it was only in the bathrooms and hall."

"Because we wouldn't have been able to find a match."

"Your papa found that tile. He looked for weeks to find the perfect one."

"Yeah, I know." Just like Javy knew he could look forever and not find the perfect match. He'd already tried to explain about different dye lots, about the Saltillo's finish aging over time, about manufacturers discontinuing styles.

But, then, this wasn't about tile or even about the restaurant. This was about his father's dedication and commitment, qualities that had made him the love of Maria's life. Even after ten years, she remained fiercely loyal to her husband's memory. It was a devotion that left Javy in awe and wondering what it would be like to have a woman love him like that.

To have *Emily* love him like that.

The thought should have come from left field, blindsiding him and knocking him on his ass. Instead, the idea whispered through his mind like it had been there all along. And wasn't that what remodeling the restaurant was really about for him? To prove he not only had what it took to see things through, but that he deserved a woman who would stay by his side…

He probably couldn't pick a worse time to talk to Maria, but this was his last chance. Either they started the remodel or they went ahead and planned for the reopening next Saturday. Once the restaurant was up and running, it would take another disaster for Maria to close the doors again.

"It's a big change, but I think you'll be glad once it's done. Just like I think you'd like the changes if we remodeled the patio and bar. I get that it's hard to take that first step but—"

"No, Javier. You do not *get it*. Not if you think I would ever be happy to see Delgado's change. You look around and see someplace old-fashioned and out of date. I see the *restaurante* exactly as it was when my Miguel last walked through those doors."

Maria flung a hand toward the lobby. Javy's gaze automatically followed, and a slight movement caught his eye.

"So, no, Javier. No more changes." Maria spun on a heel at her final word and disappeared out the back as suddenly as she'd arrived. And the silence he had enjoyed as such a peaceful relief only moments ago was now filled with frustration and regret.

"You can come out, Emily," he said, glancing toward the lobby, where he'd spotted her seconds earlier.

Stepping into the dining area, Emily wished she'd given in to the urge to slip away unnoticed. She hadn't intended to eavesdrop but hadn't thought anything of it when she heard voices coming from the restaurant. At Maria's outburst, though, Emily had frozen in place. Last thing she'd wanted to do was to interrupt, but she'd been equally afraid to call attention to herself by trying to sneak away.

She was still caught in her own indecision when Maria stormed out of the restaurant.

"I'm sorry, Javy. I wasn't trying to eavesdrop—"

"But you heard everything."

"Enough," she admitted. Enough to know how hurt he must be by his mother's refusal to trust in the changes he wanted to make, and enough to realize now why Maria was so against those changes.

"She must have really loved your dad."

"More than anything," he agreed, the flatness in the words telling Emily more than he was willing to say. He leaned against the handle of the push broom, but the defeat she saw in his posture had nothing to do with the long, hard days of physical labor he'd put in.

"Javy…"

"Look, let's just forget about this."

A part of Emily was tempted to do just that. The part of her that didn't cause waves, that never mentioned touchy subjects, that pasted on a happy face and let things slide…

Except that part of her was becoming smaller and smaller, and it was Javy who had encouraged her to stand up for herself, to speak out. And this was her chance to stand up and speak out—for him.

"This isn't about you. You must know that. Your mother is trying to hold on to the past and the memory of your father."

"That's not the only past she's holding on to."

Anna's insight—that Maria wouldn't change her opinion of Javy until he changed his ways—echoed in Emily's thoughts, but she wasn't about to repeat his cousin's words. First, she didn't know if the other woman was right, and second, because Javy was…Javy. Charming, flirtatious, sexy, and Emily didn't want him to change.

"I wanted to prove I could do this. That I deserve…"

His voice trailed off, but the look of longing in his dark eyes reached out and squeezed Emily's heart, reminding her there was more to Javy than his charm and sex appeal. He did a good job of hiding it, and Emily did her best not to see it, because that was the side of Javy she was coming dangerously close to falling for.

"Javy…"

He quickly shook his head, denying anything she might have seen. "It doesn't matter. She doesn't trust me, and she has every right not to."

"That's not true," Emily protested. "Why would you even say that?"

"Maybe because she can't forget that I practically destroyed the place the first time she left me in charge." Javy let go of the broom, and it fell to the bare concrete floor with a loud clatter.

"What are you talking about? When did…" Emily's voice trailed away as she guessed the answer in the pointed look he gave her. "The fire ten years ago."

"I was in charge that night. I'm the reason Connor took money from your family and left town."

Emily didn't know if Maria truly blamed Javy for the long-ago accident, but she had no doubt that it *was* an accident. And whatever guilt Javy felt, she refused to add to it. Especially over a relationship with Connor that would never have lasted, anyway.

She longed to reach out to him and offer what comfort she could, but the tension pulling at his shoulders and knotting the ropelike muscles in his arms told Emily he wouldn't accept her consolation. He would likely see her sympathy as pity and reject any overture she made.

Taking a chance and hoping it didn't backfire, she changed tactics. She stepped closer and canted her head in challenge. "So, what you're saying is that…" Emily paused. "You owe me."

Javy blinked once and then a second time before the edge of guilt and regret disappeared from his dark eyes. "I think, technically, I owe your parents."

"Hmm, considering that I'm planning to make you work off your debt, I think you'd much rather owe me."

He crossed his arms over his chest, hiding a would-be

smile behind a dark frown. "Gotta tell you, I don't like being indebted to anyone. So what exactly do you have in mind?"

"Dinner," Emily said, before quickly adding, "Tomorrow night." He'd been hard at work all day, and she wanted to give them both something to look forward to.

"Just dinner?" he asked, an obvious dare written in his voice.

"It was ten thousand dollars, Javy," she deadpanned. "It better be more than just dinner."

"I'd say that you're playing with fire, but considering the circumstances…"

"Good point."

He let loose the smile he'd been fighting, his white teeth flashing in his too-handsome face, and shook his head. "Now I know what you mean."

"Excuse me?"

"The night of the wedding, when you said I could make you laugh when you didn't even feel like smiling. Now I know how that feels—thanks to you."

Pleasure poured through her, and for a split second, Emily thought maybe she should worry that making Javy smile, making him laugh, made her so ridiculously happy. But as soon as it formed, she brushed the concern aside. She was *not* going to freak herself out over how *happy* she was! So maybe it wouldn't last, all the more reason to enjoy the feeling now.

"So I guess that's one I owed you," she teased.

Javy smiled again, but she could see the toll the day of hard work and harder words had taken on him. The shadows beneath his eyes competed with the shadow of his beard. More than once he'd twitched his right arm and shoulder, trying to stretch out some stiffness, and numerous nicks and scrapes marked his hands.

"I should let you go… It's getting late," she murmured.

"Yeah," he agreed, but he didn't make any sudden move to leave. "I'd love a cold beer and a hot tub right now."

The heat in his dark eyes told Emily that wasn't *all* he wished for. She swallowed against a suddenly dry throat, which could have used a cold beer of its own, even as she took a step toward the door. As tempting as the idea of slipping into a tub of hot water on a hotter night was, the timing wasn't right. The day had been filled with too much emotional upheaval to think it wouldn't carry over. And besides...

"I'll see you tomorrow night," she promised.

Javy nodded. "Tomorrow night," he echoed, only to call her name before she reached the door. "I didn't even think to ask earlier, but why did you come back?"

Hardly able to believe she'd forgotten, Emily stopped short and flashed a smile over her shoulder. "Anna called. The buyer accepted my offer on the town house."

"Hey, that's great! When Anna said there was another offer, I was afraid you might miss out."

"So was I."

She very nearly had, thanks to old insecurities and old habits holding her back. But she'd learned her lesson. She refused to let her fears rob her of this time with Javy. It had been only one day, and she'd missed him terribly. Each breath she took had scraped the raw emptiness inside her. Now, though, after seeing him again, she realized that place in her chest didn't feel so empty. Instead, her heart was practically bursting with happiness, excitement and a heady, overwhelming emotion she refused to name....

But something of those feelings must have shown in her expression, plain as day, for Javy to read. "Tomorrow night," he echoed again, his voice a husky, sensual promise that Emily could no longer wait for him to fulfill.

Chapter Nine

Emily watched with a smile as Angela Delgado looked through the rainbow of skirts, blouses, dresses and slacks laid out on her king-size bed. The woman gaped and offered prayers in Spanish beneath her breath as she ran her hands over the various fabrics. Emily knew without a doubt that Anna's mother was taking more pleasure in simply *looking* at the clothes than she ever had in wearing them.

"*All* of these?" Angela questioned for the third time, as if she feared the colorful bounty spread over the cream-colored bedspread would be suddenly taken away.

"All of them," Emily reiterated.

Once she'd learned her offer for the town house had been accepted, she'd wasted no time in arranging for Angela to come look at the clothes.

Still buried wrist-deep in designer outfits, Angela said, "Lauren will love these. I asked her to stop by. That is okay?"

"Yes, of course."

Emily had barely said the words when she heard a soft knock on the open bedroom door. A wide-eyed young woman with short brown hair stuck her head inside. "Sorry I'm late. I didn't think I was at the right house and…"

The woman—Lauren, Emily assumed—went completely silent when she saw the turquoise cashmere sweater Angela held up. "Is that… Are these the clothes?" she asked, her voice barely above a whisper.

"Whatever you like," Emily offered.

"Lauren just got a job with a law firm," the older woman said, as much pride shining in her eyes as when she talked about her daughter, Anna.

"I'm only the receptionist," Lauren clarified quietly.

"It is a good job, a professional job, and you need to look the part," said Angela.

Emily nodded her agreement. "By the time we're done, you'll have the perfect business wardrobe, and maybe a few outfits for fun on a Friday night."

Lauren gave a soft laugh as she fingered the sleeve of an emerald-green silk blouse. "Somehow I don't think I'll find a jogging suit and spit-up rag in here. My idea of a fun Friday night is playing with my two-year-old son." A mother's joy lighting her expression and adding a soft beauty to her otherwise plain features, she asked, "Would you like to see a picture?"

When Emily nodded, Lauren pulled out her wallet and showed photos of a chubby-faced, smiling toddler.

"He's beautiful," Emily declared.

"He's what I work for, why I want a better life. And I'm so lucky to have found Angela. She helped me get this job. If not for her…" Lauren's voice trailed off. She didn't even want to mention what her fate might have been.

"You don't have any family who can help you?" Emily asked.

Running her thumb over her son's face, the young woman shook her head. "I was a senior in high school when I met Ben's father. My parents didn't like him. They said he was a user, told me to stay away from him. Obviously, I didn't listen," she said with a wry smile as she tucked the photos and wallet away. "I ran off to be with him. Only, my parents ended up being right, but by then it was too late. I was pregnant, and as far as my family was concerned, I'd made my decision, and I had to live with it."

At eighteen, Emily had done the same thing—defied her parents and snuck behind their backs to date Connor. What would have happened had she run off with him, only to come home pregnant and alone? She tried to imagine her parents turning their backs on her but couldn't. Their disappointment and disapproval would have been a heavy burden to bear, but she knew they loved her enough to welcome her back home.

Where they would have used her past mistakes to keep her firmly in line.

Emily tried to shove aside the unkind thought, but she knew the truth, just like she knew without a doubt that her parents would see her relationship with Javy as a mistake.

But from now on, she was playing by her own rules and doing what she wanted. And even though any relationship with Javy was bound to be short-lived, she planned to enjoy every minute. Beginning with their date that night.

"Maybe this one. Or this…"

Emily turned her attention back to the two women, who were having a hard time matching up the different pieces into coordinating outfits. Reaching past them and into the closet, she pulled out a pair of charcoal gray slacks to go with the turquoise sweater. "Here. Try this."

Seconds later, Lauren stepped out of the bathroom to model her new clothes. "What do you think?"

Looking at Lauren, Emily tried not to smile. The two pieces combined made a lovely outfit, but the sleeves slid past Lauren's fingertips, and she stood in a pool of gray wool. With her delicate features and short hair, she looked like a little girl playing dress up.

Emily tilted her head. "I think it will be a wonderful outfit once it's tailored—"

"She can roll up the sleeves of the sweater, and a hem will do fine for the pants," the older woman insisted, not refusing Emily's advice as much as admitting a hem was the best she could do.

But to truly fit correctly, the outfit needed more than a simple hem....

"You know, my cousin has a friend who's a dress designer," said Emily. "She went to a local fashion institute, and I remember her saying she spent hours learning how to tailor clothes. I wonder if we could arrange for some of the current students to alter the clothes for extra credit."

"Do you think they would?" Lauren asked.

The hope shining in her eyes made Emily wish she'd never said a word. What did she know about what the design students could or couldn't do? She shouldn't have gotten Lauren's hopes up when she had no idea....

"Perfect!" Angela exclaimed. "Emily, you will arrange this for us, yes?"

With both women looking at her with such expectation, what else could she say but...yes.

After Angela and Lauren left, their arms weighed down with bags stuffed with clothes, Emily gathered the many now-empty hangers. She hadn't expected to enjoy the afternoon as much as she had, but the women had given Emily's spirits a lift she hadn't even realized she needed.

Wondering what more she could do to help the charity, Emily didn't notice that her mother had entered the bedroom until Charlene said, "I saw those two women as they were leaving. Do you have any clothes left?"

"Of course." Emily crossed her arms at her waist. She hated that every conversation with her parents right now turned into an argument. Why couldn't they be happy for her? Or, if that was too much to expect, couldn't they at least respect her decision to move out?

Instead, she felt like she had when she was five and cut her own hair. For weeks her mother had shaken her head in a combination of disappointment and hope that her scalped bangs would grow out before anyone noticed.

Emily met that same look in her mother's eyes now, as if she were making some foolish mistake that Charlene was hoping she would quickly grow out of.

Replacing the empty hangers on the rod, Emily said, "The things I gave away were outfits I haven't worn in months, and they are all going to a good cause."

Lauren had hugged Emily before she left, the shy, awkward embrace revealing that she wasn't accustomed to such displays of affection. "Only a few months ago, I prayed for someone to help me and my son," the young woman had whispered. "First, I found Angela, and now, you. I can't thank you enough, Emily."

Emily had never been the answer to *anything* before, and she couldn't stop thinking about the light in Lauren's eyes as she tried on one outfit after another. Even though the clothes hadn't been perfect fits, it had been like watching an impromptu fashion show.

Donating more clothes would help the charity, but was there some way to combine the clothes and the fashion show into some kind of money-raising opportunity? An event where everyday women, not high-paid models, walked the catwalk and the clothes worn were donated items instead of haute couture originals?

Caught up in the possibilities, Emily almost missed what her mother was saying until two words struck out at her.

"I've decided to have Dan Rogers's dinner party next weekend."

"Next weekend?" The Delgado's reopening was that same weekend, an event she was looking forward to almost as much as she was dreading her mother's dinner party. "What night?"

Charlene frowned. "Friday. Why?"

Breathing a sigh of relief, Emily said, "I have plans on Saturday and I was worried…."

"Worried what?" her mother asked, expectation written in the lift of her eyebrows.

Obviously Charlene thought her dinner party superseded any plans Emily might have made. "I was worried there might be a conflict, but there isn't." Trying to summon up a proper amount of interest, she asked, "How many people will be attending?"

"Six. I was thinking of having a seafood theme—lobster bisque, crab legs…."

"Hmm, my favorites."

"It turns out seafood is Dan's favorite, too."

They spoke for a few more minutes, discussing whether or not to have the meal catered or to bring in a personal chef, as well as what desserts might be on the menu.

"Am I keeping you from something?" her mother asked, catching Emily glancing at the bedside clock and pinning her to the spot with a pointed look.

Emily had known this conversation was coming. If she was going to make her own choices, then she was going to have to learn to accept her parents' disapproval. Ignoring the nerves turning her insides into origami, she said, "I have a date tonight."

"A date? With whom?"

"Javier Delgado. He was Connor's best man, and they've been friends for years."

Her mother's frown told Emily that while Charlene might have reluctantly welcomed Connor into the family, the same invitation didn't extend to his friends. "Emily, are you sure you're ready for this? What do you even know about this man?"

She shrugged. "I know I like being with him."

"If you want to go out, your father and I know plenty of young men from good families—"

"Men like Todd?" Emily couldn't help asking.

Charlene flinched. "Is that what this is about? Moving, giving away your clothes, going out with this man... Are you punishing us for not protecting you from Todd?"

"No. Of course not. Todd fooled all of us, but he's the only one to blame for that." And she could only blame herself for letting things go as far as they had. "It's not your fault, and I shouldn't have brought him up."

"I'm glad you did, Emily. I'm sure this experience with Todd has shown you that there are men in the world who will use you to get what they want...."

Knowing where her mother was going, Emily shook her head. "Not Javy."

"How do you know?"

"Because he told me..." He'd also told her she needed to confront her parents.

Taking a deep breath, she said, "He told me he wouldn't take money from our family again."

"Again?"

"The money you gave Connor to leave town..." Her mother recoiled at the reminder. "He gave it to the Delgados to save their restaurant."

"And what exactly did he hope to gain by telling you that?"

"Nothing. He thought I already knew," Emily replied pointedly.

Charlene sighed. "After Connor left, your father and I didn't see any reason to tell you."

"Not telling me is the least of the problem! Why couldn't you… Why haven't you *ever* trusted me to make my own decisions?"

"Including the decision to run off with a man your father and I disapproved of when you were eighteen?"

"This goes back so much further than Connor. I feel like I've spent my whole life with you and Daddy watching over my shoulder, just waiting for me to repeat some *huge* mistake!"

"That's ridiculous," Charlene insisted, even as she rubbed a spot on her crystal watch face and refused to meet Emily's gaze.

"No, it's not." She wasn't being ridiculous, but she couldn't force her mother to talk. "Although it is almost funny. You don't even trust me enough to tell me why you don't trust me. Now, if you'll excuse me, I have to get ready for my date."

As Emily turned toward the bathroom, Charlene called out her name. Looking back, Emily could see the debate playing out behind her mother's normally reserved features. She waited, hoping her mother might finally open up, but at the last moment Charlene said, "Everything your father and I have done has been in your best interests. We never wanted to hurt you."

Frustrated by an explanation that didn't explain anything, Emily nodded. Her parents did love her. She had no doubt of that. She could only hope they would understand that, from now on, as much as she loved them, as much she didn't want to hurt them, she could look out for herself.

Javy had everything set for his date with Emily, and he was looking forward to the evening with an eagerness fitting for a first date—if he were thirteen and this were his first date *ever.*

For a grown man with his experience, this should have been a typical night. But he couldn't ignore the feeling that if he let it, this could be more....

Doing his best to shake it off, he just grabbed his keys. He was heading for the door when his cell phone rang. He answered the call as he hit the button for the garage.

"Hey, it's Anna," his cousin responded to his greeting. "I talked to my mom a few minutes ago, and she is thrilled. She said Emily gave the charity a ton of clothes."

Javy listened with half an ear as his cousin raved about fashion. He had already backed down the driveway and pulled onto the street before Anna switched gears to the Wilsons' house.

"And she says the house is a mansion, with these amazing columns and this huge fountain out front!"

"Yeah? Well, I guess I'll see for myself tonight, when I pick Emily up for our date."

"Are you sure that's a good idea?"

"If this is about Emily and Stephanie being too much alike, you're wrong."

Expecting an argument, Anna surprised him by saying, "I know. I misjudged her. Emily's stronger than I thought, and she's a woman who knows what she wants."

"I thought so from the moment I met her." He was glad other people were starting to see the strength beneath Emily's beauty. He hoped Emily was starting to see it herself.

"Which brings me back to my question… Are you sure dating Emily is a good idea, considering your track record?"

His hand tightened on the wheel as he stopped at a red light. "So I've dated a lot of women. What's wrong with that?"

"Nothing if you're nineteen, but you aren't."

At nineteen, he'd been reeling from his father's death, nursing a broken heart, thanks to Stephanie's desertion, and struggling to make ends meet at the restaurant. Dating had been the last thing on his mind, and okay, so maybe playing the field had been a way of making up for lost time, but still...

"Isn't that better than getting serious about a woman when I'm not interested in marriage?" he asked, even as he wondered if the old excuse still rang true.

"And what about Emily?"

"Emily wants to have a good time. To branch out and spread her wings. She ended an engagement days before her wedding. Believe me, she's not looking for anything serious."

Which was probably the only reason she was with him, Javy thought, feeling somewhat grim at the realization.

"Emily wants to get married and have a family."

"What?" The light turned green, and Javy hit the gas hard enough to send his tires squealing, but zero to sixty couldn't outrun the speed of sound or his cousin's voice. "She said that?"

"She didn't have to, Javy. She was days away from getting married before the wedding was called off. Doesn't that tell you anything?"

"Yeah, it tells me Emily was about to make a huge mistake, and she's lucky Connor was there to stop her."

The silence from the other end of the line told Javy his response wasn't what his cousin wanted to hear. The chill in her voice confirmed that thought when she said, "I guess it's unfortunate Connor isn't here now, isn't it?"

Anna's words were still ringing in his thoughts when he stepped inside the Wilsons' house a half an hour later. Her mother hadn't exaggerated when she'd called the place a mansion. Following the maid through the travertine foyer, he felt like he was walking through a museum. Gorgeous vases rested on carved pedestals, sculptures posed in backlit niches, and the walls were decorated with floor-to-ceiling paintings.

The museum-like feel continued as he stepped inside a

study, not so much because of the room's mahogany and leather furnishings, but because of the way Gordon Wilson, seated behind an enormous desk, stared at him as if he expected Javy to run off with the *Mona Lisa*.

Javy hadn't arrived at this meeting unprepared, but his conversation with Anna had left him feeling off balance. Was his cousin right? Did Emily want commitment, marriage and family, everything he'd avoided for the past ten years?

Or maybe the more important question was, did she want those things from him?

"Your friend Connor sat in here a week ago," Gordon said without preamble. "We were both relieved Emily escaped marriage to a man who would have hurt her."

"I'm not out to hurt Emily," Javy insisted, wondering which of them he was trying to convince. If he couldn't give Emily the family and life she wanted, he should begin laying the groundwork for backing off now. He should let Gordon Wilson think what he would and start making his excuses to Emily for not seeing her again.

He never walked into a situation without establishing a way out. He knew all the escape routes. Work, family, he had the emergency excuses down pat. With the women he dated, he rarely needed them, but like a flight attendant discussing water landings for trips over desert-dry areas, his excuses were still at the ready.

And yet the thought of letting Emily go threatened to carve out all the anticipation, joy and excitement from his life, leaving him…leaving him in the same shape he'd been in after Stephanie ran off.

Seeing the doubt written as clearly as the lines forming on the older man's forehead, Javy took a deep breath and decided to lay all his cards on the table. "I'm not Emily's ex-fiancé. I don't have a pregnant girlfriend on the side, and I'm not interested in your money. In fact, I think this is the perfect time to give you this."

Pulling out his wallet, he withdrew a folded piece of paper and flipped it onto the leather blotter on Gordon Wilson's desk.

The older man's silvered eyebrows rose. "What is it?"

"A check," Javy stated. "For ten thousand dollars. I figure when my friend Connor sat in this chair a week ago, he didn't bother to tell you he gave me your payoff money to save my family's restaurant. He only recently told me, and since he's never let me repay him, no matter how many times I've tried, I figure I'll repay you."

He could joke with Emily about working off his debt, but he didn't like owing anyone. He'd let it go as long as he had when Connor held his marker, but not now. Not when Gordon Wilson—Emily's father—had been the one to sign over the cash.

Gordon deliberately unfolded the check, no doubt making sure it wasn't made of rubber. His granite features revealed nothing as he set it aside. "Is this supposed to prove something?"

"Only that you won't be able to buy me off."

"Unfortunately, it will take more than that—" Gordon jerked a stubborn, bearded chin toward the check "—to convince me you won't end up hurting my daughter."

Chapter Ten

"I'm sorry you were stuck talking to my father for so long," Emily apologized as Javy turned the car along the Wilsons' circular driveway and through the gated exit.

Dressed in a denim-colored halter dress that left the creamy skin of her shoulders and back gloriously bare, Emily shifted on the passenger seat to face him. She crossed one leg over the other, drawing his attention to even more bare skin and a pair of beaded, strappy sandals, which made it almost impossible for Javy to keep his eyes on the road.

"You were worth the wait. You look amazing," he told her, the flattery coming as easily as breathing.

And although the words had never been so true, the flirting that had been a part of his dating routine for so long suddenly felt as tired and worn as his oldest beat-up pair of jeans. Looking into Emily's turquoise eyes, Javy couldn't help wondering if maybe, just maybe, it was time for something new.

"You would think clearing out my closet like I did today would make things easier to find, but...no," she said with a smile as she ran her fingers along the dress's hemline just below her knees. Even though there was nothing purposefully seductive in the simple move, Javy felt his mouth go as dry as the parched desert landscape surrounding them.

"I talked to Anna earlier." The mere mention of his cousin had her voice ringing in his head, reminding him of all the things Emily wanted, all the things he wasn't sure he could give, but he did his best to shove them aside. "She says my aunt Angela's pretty excited about all the clothes you gave her."

"I was glad to help. I, um, was thinking that if I could get some students at the fashion institute involved, they could alter the donated clothes."

"Sounds like a great idea."

Emily sighed even as she fiddled with the zipper on her beaded purse, a sure sign of nerves. "I only wish someone else had come up with that great idea. Instead, I started talking without thinking, and now Angela is counting on me."

"You can do this, Emily. You know you can."

She laughed softly. "I don't know how you do it."

"Do what?"

"Make me believe in myself even when no one else will."

Stopped at a red light, he glanced over at her. Even though the sun was setting behind her, when Emily smiled, it was the light coming from inside her that nearly blinded him. The pleasure she took in his faith in her, so much greater than her reaction to his compliment, only served to reinforce his earlier thought.

His usual arsenal of flattery and flirting wouldn't work with Emily. She wanted, no, *deserved* more. The question was, did he have it in himself to give?

The thought of reaching out and opening up after so many

years of holding back left him feeling vulnerable, exposed. The last time he'd opened up his heart to a woman, he'd had it ripped from his chest.

And he didn't think surviving that would be any easier the second time around.

Unaware of the reservations swirling through him, Emily went on with her ideas for his aunt's charity. "A girl named Lauren came to the house with your aunt. Seeing her model the clothes made me think of having a fashion show. Only instead of models wearing famous designer originals, anyone who wanted to volunteer could show off their own style and then donate those outfits at the end of the night."

Emily's voice started picking up speed and strength the more she talked, and Javy knew she'd given the concept a great deal of thought.

"I also wanted to have Lauren and the other women at the shelter involved. If the students from the fashion institute help, we could show some before shots and then have the women model the clothes after they've been tailored to fit them. Of course, there would be auction items to help raise money and…" Her voice trailed off. "See? I'm totally getting ahead of myself. I have no idea if the students would be willing to volunteer. Cassie—my friend with the jewelry boutique—and I could lend the women all the accessories they'd need for the fashion show, as well as donate some items for an auction, but I don't have any idea who else would be willing—"

"Hey, I would," he interrupted, hating to see her excitement denied by self-doubt. "Dinner for two at the restaurant. Best table in the house."

"Really?"

"Yeah. It's for a good cause, and my aunt would kick my butt if I didn't."

"That's…that means a lot to me. Thank you, Javy."

He glanced her way again and hoped that it was only a trick of the setting sun that was making her eyes look like they were shining. The thought of Emily crying, even grateful tears, hit like a below-the-belt blow.

He wasn't used to women crying in his presence. He always made sure his dates had a good time, always made sure to leave them with a smile, always made sure to date only women who knew the rules and how he played. Most of them were better at the game than he was, and no way did those women cry.

But Emily was different. He'd spotted it the moment he saw her at the reception that should have been hers, trying so hard to show everyone how little she cared about her broken dreams. Yet he'd still asked her out.

Because he'd thought she was looking for a good time, Javy argued, for a man to build her confidence back up and reinforce that she was a sexy, desirable woman. And he was the man for the job….

Only what if he was wrong and Anna was right? What if Emily *did* want more than a good time? Nerves clawing at his gut, his hands tightened on the wheel. What if *he* wanted more than a good time?

"Javy, is everything all right?" Emily asked quietly, breaking the silence.

"What? Yeah. Why?"

"You got really quiet. You haven't said anything for three miles."

"Sorry. I was just thinking."

"How's everything at the restaurant? Do you think you'll make Alex's schedule for the reopening?"

"I think so. Tomorrow we'll get started on the drywall and baseboard repairs and start installing the tile. Alex says that it'll take only three days, but we'll see."

"I'm looking forward to tasting some of your favorite dishes." As Javy turned into a residential neighborhood, Emily added, "And speaking of eating, you haven't told me where we're going for dinner tonight."

"That's because I was keeping it a surprise," he said.

He flashed her a smile, but even in the fading daylight, Emily sensed that something was missing. He hadn't seemed himself since picking her up. She wondered if her father had said something to him, but Javy hardly seemed the type to be intimidated by anyone, even a man like her father. And yet everything had been fine when she left the restaurant last night…hadn't it?

Turning her attention back to the conversation, she asked, "And how long do you plan to keep me in suspense?"

"Not much longer, since we're here." Javy pulled into the driveway of a flat-roofed, adobe-style house.

"Where is here?"

"My house. I wanted to take you out for the best meal you've ever had, but I won't be able to do that until the restaurant is back up and running. So, for now, you'll have the next best thing."

He climbed from the car and circled around to open the door for her before adding, "A home-cooked meal by me."

"I suppose I shouldn't be surprised that you cook," Emily said, following Javy along a path lined with mosaic tiles toward the front door. The instant she stepped inside, she was hit by a burst of air-conditioned air scented with mouthwatering peppers, onions and spices she couldn't name.

Leading the way through a comfortable living room filled with overstuffed, man-size leather furniture and a large flat-screen television to an eat-in kitchen, Javy said, "According to my mother, cooking is as important as eating. If you can't do one, how can you do the other?"

"Not a lot of ordering takeout in the Delgado household, huh?" Emily teased as she perched on a bar stool, resting her elbows on the brown and-gold-flecked countertop, while Javy stepped up to the stove.

He picked up a wooden spoon, which looked as comfortable in his hand as the hammer and chisel she'd seen him use, and lifted the lid off a slow-cooker. He gave a stir and declared the tortilla soup almost ready. He pulled a platter of chopped peppers and onions from the refrigerator and started them sizzling in a frying pan before saying, "I can't tell you what a treat it was when I'd spend the night at a friend's house, and we'd go out for pizza or hamburgers. Man, I thought Happy Meals were the best. I had no idea how good I had it."

"I guess we all take the people around us for granted." After telling Javy about how Lauren and her son were on their own, with no help from Lauren's family, Emily said, "There's no way my family would ever just…disown me like that."

"But you never challenged your parents like that, either," Javy said. "Not for long," he added when he realized she might bring up her short-lived, defiant relationship with Connor.

He didn't ask, but Emily read the curiosity written in his dark eyes. Why had she always done what she was told? Why had she put so much more importance on making everyone else happy instead of making herself happy?

Watching him gather avocados, an onion, garlic, jalapeños, a lime and tomatoes from the corner of the counter, ingredients even she recognized as the makings for guacamole, Emily tried to put her jumbled thoughts into words. "I guess, maybe, it's like you using fresh fruit and vegetables. That's what your mother thought was the right thing to do. It probably would have been easier and maybe cheaper to use canned or frozen or dried ingredients. But you're making dinner the way she taught you without even thinking about it."

And doing an impressive job. He handled a knife with the kind of skill she'd only witnessed on TV. He had the onion and tomatoes chopped, the peppers and garlic diced, and the avocados scooped from their skins and sprinkled with lime juice in less time than it would have taken her to get the skin off a single garlic clove. Without even measuring or checking a recipe once.

After so many years, making her parents happy had gotten to be the same thing—something she did out of habit without every stopping to wonder why. "My parents always taught me that they knew best, that their ideas were better than mine. Somehow I fell into the habit of doing as I was told and convinced myself that as long as my parents were happy, I would be happy."

"But you weren't." The words were a statement, not a question, but Emily answered, anyway.

"No. And now that I'm trying to live my own life and make my own decisions, it's still hard when I feel like I'm disappointing them."

"They aren't disappointed, just surprised and maybe a little worried. You've changed the rules of a lifetime. You need to give them a chance to catch up."

"Yeah? How long do you think it would take your mother to get used to the idea of you using guacamole that came from a jar?"

The corners of his mouth kicked up at her point. "Okay, that would never happen, but it isn't the same thing. My mother and I might not agree on everything, but she's right about the fresh vegetables." He finished mixing the ingredients, added a dash of salt and pepper, and grabbed a tortilla chip from a nearby bag. Scooping up a dollop of guacamole, he circled the island and held it out for her to taste. "Fresh really is the best. See for yourself."

She could have reached out and taken the chip, but the glint in his dark eyes was a challenge she couldn't resist. Leaning forward, she tasted the sample he offered straight from his hand. The flavors exploded against her tongue—the crisp tortilla, the cool, smooth avocado, the crunch of onion, and bite of pepper, all in perfect combination.

But the second he brushed his fingers against her lips, she could have been eating cardboard for all she cared, and the only taste she craved was his kiss.

His eyes darkened to onyx as he focused on the slow stroke of his thumb against her lower lip. Anticipation beat like the relentless thump of bass in her chest, loud enough and strong enough that she expected the windows to tremble from the reverberations.

But Javy still didn't kiss her. Like a gourmet drawing out the appetizers and salad to whet the appetite for the main course, he only teased her. He trailed his fingers along her jaw before he cupped the nape of her neck.

The contact of his skin against hers sent her blood sizzling, snapping and popping in her veins like the vegetables sautéing on the stove. All before he'd even kissed her. He stepped closer until the heat from his body surrounded her and finally, *finally,* claimed her mouth with his own.

But if the wait had filled Emily with anticipation, it had let something loose inside of Javy.

This was nothing like the practiced seduction the night of the wedding or the kisses where he'd allowed her the pretense of control. This kiss was wild, unpredictable, hotter and better than anything that had come before. His fingers tangled in her hair as her head fell back with a moan. His denim-clad legs brushed against hers as he pressed closer. The edge of the island countertop bumped against the small of her back, but instead of feeling trapped, she was aware that the solid surface was the only thing keeping her upright as her world tilted off its axis.

Her hands swam from the small of his back, to his hips, his sides. The soft cotton slid over his skin, conforming to muscle and bone, but Emily wanted more. Inching up the material, her fingers found the hem of his shirt and dove beneath. His skin was silky smooth and hot against her hands, but it wasn't enough. She wanted more, the pulse of desire low in her belly telling her she wanted everything.

Javy breathed her name against skin as his mouth trailed from her cheek to her ear to her throat until Emily's head swam from the sheer pleasure. Each time she sucked in a much-needed breath, her breasts brushed against his chest, stealing the air from her lungs all over again in a delicious circle she never wanted to end….

The shrill blast of an alarm sliced through the air, severing the connection that had been so strong seconds before. Javy jumped back and swore as his gaze locked on the smoking peppers and onions. Color washed from his face even as his jaw clenched hard enough to crack his back teeth.

Still reeling from the kiss, Emily couldn't seem to make herself move on legs that felt as wilted as whatever was left of the vegetables. "Javy—"

"I've got it," he bit out. In two steps he dumped the pan in the sink, turned on the water and hit the switch to start the exhaust fan over the stove whirling.

The fire alarm sputtered, then quit after a final bleat or two, leaving a smoky silence to fill the kitchen.

Emily's heart was still pounding in her throat, limiting her breaths to quick pants, but with a rough shake of his head, Javy seemed to dismiss everything that had just happened: the kiss, the smoke alarm and his reaction to it.

"Sorry about that." He ran a hand through his hair, smoothing out the rough edges left by her fingers and smothering the flames. "When I said I wanted to show off my skill in the kitchen, flambé wasn't what I had in mind. You better go have a seat before this kitchen goes up in smoke."

"You could always take the other pot off the stove," she suggested hopefully.

"It's not the stove I'm worried about," he said, the heat in his eyes making her feel like *she* was on fire.

But instead of kissing her again, he took a step back. "Give me another few minutes and dinner will be ready."

Emily nodded, but Javy didn't notice. He'd already turned away, leaving her to stare at his broad back and wish she could turn back time.

Had anyone asked, Javy would have sworn he didn't have a seduction routine. That every woman was different and therefore every date was different. But only now, seated at the table across from Emily, did he realize the one thing that was always the same—him. Whether he took his date out for a night on the town, hopping from one Scottsdale club to another, or out to some five-star restaurant or on a picnic by the lake, *he* never changed.

"I'm thinking that I've been somewhat monopolizing our conversations. You know all about me, and I don't know nearly as much about you," Emily said.

They'd just finished dinner, and Emily's voice had an overly bright quality, as if he should expect to see a TV camera or microphone nearby. His fault, he knew, because of the silence that had fallen between them after he'd pulled away from that kiss instead of taking things a step further.

It was what he would have done any other night of the week, with any other woman. But he'd never lost control like he did with Emily. A part of him always knew what he was doing at any given moment in any given relationship.

To completely lose it with Emily was unacceptable. To completely lose it and almost start another freakin' fire was like fate slapping him upside the head. Reminding him of what could happen if he let himself get distracted. Of how much he could lose.

He needed to get back in control. To keep things light, fun, free of the heavy emotions that always bogged relationships down. Not an easy thing to do when the reminder of how completely he'd lost it still filled the house with the faint smell of smoke.

"You know I'm friends with Connor," he pointed out, forcing his thoughts back to the conversation. "You've met some of my family. You've been to the restaurant."

"And you know that I've let my parents dictate my entire life, that I nearly married a man I didn't love to please them and that my former fiancé proposed only to try and get into his family's good graces after getting their maid pregnant. I'd say you have the upper hand."

He didn't want that, not when he knew Emily had spent most of her life feeling that way, but he didn't want to spill his guts like he'd suddenly found himself on *Dr. Phil,* either.

And yet wouldn't Emily expect that? For him to express his *feelings?* To be open and honest and reveal all the emotional scars he'd kept hidden for so long? To talk about Stephanie, his father and the fire at the restaurant, all the things he'd done his best to ignore for years?

His muscles already tensing, he asked, "What do you want to know?"

Resting her chin on her interlaced fingers, Emily stared at him until he actually shifted beneath her gaze. What question did she want to ask that she had to think about for so long?

Finally, she said, "I've been wondering… What's your favorite color?"

"My…what?" Javy rocked back in his chair with a startled laugh.

"Favorite color. Don't be embarrassed. Everyone has one."

She flashed a teasing grin, and even though he knew she wasn't letting him off the hook, he appreciated the brief reprieve. Looking into her gorgeous eyes, he answered, "Turquoise."

"Turquoise? Not blue? Not green?"

"Turquoise," he repeated.

"I don't think I've ever heard of that being someone's favorite color before," she mused.

"It wasn't mine until recently." He paused. "It's the color of your eyes."

"I always thought my eyes were blue," she said, slanting a seductive gaze at him from beneath her lashes.

"They are, but they have these dark specks, like the marks on a piece of turquoise, which make each stone unique, mysterious. Just like you."

A soft blush lit Emily's cheeks, and her teasing smile faded away. For a moment, everything faded away until it was only the two of them and nothing more existed beyond their focus on one another. "I, um…what about music?"

Javy shrugged. "All kinds. Especially songs you can dance to."

"And I should know. You're a really good dancer."

"My mother taught me when I was a kid. She thought it was something every young man should know how to do."

Not that Javy followed her rules. He certainly hadn't obeyed Maria's rule of maintaining a proper distance. But keeping any kind of distance had been the last thing on his mind when he'd held Emily in his arms. It had taken all his willpower not to crush her body to his until nothing—not space, not breathing room—nothing separated them.

Something of his thoughts must have showed in his face, or maybe her own memories of the dance made Emily's breath catch. "I don't know about every young man, but I can guarantee that you are the only man who could have gotten me to dance in front of all those people at what should have been my wedding."

The only man... It had been a long time since he'd been a woman's *only.* He'd fooled himself into believing he'd been Stephanie's only, only to find out the hard way how wrong he'd been. "Emily..."

As if sensing the turmoil inside him, she instantly changed the subject, quizzing him on movies and hobbies and sports. But when she paused a second time, Javy sensed another innocent question was not going to follow.

Leaning back in her chair, she adopted a casual air, which she didn't quite pull off, as she asked, "Any serious relationships?"

He could have lied. Could have offered a smile and given the easy too-many-women-too-little-time response, denying that Stephanie and the young, foolish boy who had loved her had ever existed. But the words he'd spoken to Emily's father rang in his head—his vow that he was nothing like Emily's fiancé.

He'd be lying to Emily and cheating her of an honest response if he told her anything but the truth.

"One," he admitted finally. "A long time ago."

Emily blinked, taken off guard, but by what, he wasn't sure—that he'd admitted to the relationship or that he'd even *had* one. "How serious?"

"We were engaged," he said.

"Oh," she said softly, sounding even more surprised. "What happened?"

"We broke up."

The three words did little to explain the whole story, and he could hardly blame Emily when she stared at him, waiting for more. "You broke up? That's it? That was the end of it?"

"Pretty much." Stephanie's running off to marry another guy had been the actual end of the relationship.

He'd been devastated, crushed by her betrayal. And he'd learned his lesson. Not to get emotionally involved, not to fall in love. To keep relationships fun and superficial and short.

It was a vow he'd kept for years…until now.

Chapter Eleven

Thanks to Todd, Emily thought, she had learned her lesson when it came to her inability to read men. Obviously she hadn't. At least not well enough to keep from getting hurt by Javier Delgado.

Not that he'd done anything to hurt her exactly. How could he have, when she hadn't seen him since their date?

They'd talked briefly by phone, with Javy explaining how busy he was getting the restaurant ready for the reopening. And she was busy, too. Emily had found a handful of design students willing to volunteer on behalf of the women's shelter and alter the donated clothes for the fashion show, while Cassie had agreed to loan the women anything they needed in the way of accessories. Angela and Lauren had been ecstatic, coordinating with other women who wanted to be their "fashion" models.

Emily had also talked to her sister. Aileen had been so in-

trigued by the idea that she'd asked several friends to partici-
pate in the show. One had even arranged for the event to be
held at a Scottsdale hotel, thanks to a last-minute cancellation.

Her tiny idea had sprouted wings and was soaring so high,
Emily was terrified to look down, too afraid she would lose
her courage and fall from the sky.

So it wasn't like Javy was the only thing on her mind or
like she had nothing better to do than spend time thinking of
him. But busy or not, she would have made time to see him.

That is, if he'd wanted to see her.

She'd sensed something was wrong when he picked her up
for their date. She still wasn't sure why they'd gotten off to a
rocky start, but by the end of the evening, she had had no
doubt why he'd pulled away.

It was all her fault.

No matter how many times she reminded herself their relationship was only fun and games and nothing to be taken
seriously, she wanted more. She longed for Javy to confide
in her the way she found it so easy to confide in him, so
she'd pushed.

Instead of letting his comment about a past engagement go,
she'd crossed a line and tried to get into his head. Because the
painful truth was, when it came to Javy, she wanted more; she
wanted everything.

She was falling for him, and there was nothing fun about it.
Especially now that she realized why he refused to commit to
a woman. He'd never gotten over his first love. His fiancée was
the only woman in his past who mattered; the string of serial
dates to follow was nothing but a symptom of heartbreak.

Somehow that made her own heart ache even worse, knowing he could love a woman, but that woman wouldn't be her.

"Is something wrong, ma'am?"

It took a moment for Emily to hear the masculine voice addressing her. She didn't know if she should be amused or offended that the young kids delivering her furniture kept calling her ma'am. Considering the way that neither one of them could hold her gaze for more than two seconds without turning red, she decided to stick with amused. "No, everything's fine."

"Then this spot's okay for the bookshelf?"

At her nod, the two guys pushed the large piece of furniture securely against the wall and left to unload something else from the truck.

Emily had always thought of buying a house as a time-consuming endeavor, but within days of the seller accepting her offer, Anna had come by with a congratulatory bouquet and a house key. She'd declared the quick closing a sign that Emily was simply meant for the town house.

Feeling somewhat dumbfounded that she'd *really* bought a house, Emily had given a quick laugh and mused, "Now what?"

Unaware that the question was rhetorical, Anna had breezily replied, "Move in! Make it yours."

And in between planning the fund-raiser and spending copious amounts of time thinking about *not* thinking about Javy, Emily had done just that with the help of movers and deliverymen.

Charlene had suggested that Emily place an order through the custom designer who'd handcrafted their furniture. She'd been more than slightly appalled when Emily shopped the stores around the mall, buying furniture available for delivery in only a few days.

"I don't understand the reason for all these rushed decisions," her mother had protested.

"I'm excited to move into my own place. And I don't see any reason to wait."

"Is that the real reason? Or are you simply afraid that if you stop to think about what you're doing, you'll change your mind?" her mother had asked.

Standing alone in the middle of her semi-furnished great room, Emily murmured, "I'm not going to change my mind."

"That's good," one of the guys grunted as he and his fellow deliveryman angled the couch through the front door. "'Cause this is really heavy."

"Oh, sorry." Stepping back to clear the way, she pointed out the spot in front of the entertainment center for the couch. She'd bought entire sets for the great room, as well as the bedrooms, so the small town house was already coming together. She had even purchased a few paintings to decorate the otherwise blank walls.

Her clothes were still boxed up in the spare bedroom, and she had yet to find the perfect places to arrange her personal touches, like her family pictures, the Swarovski crystal figurines she collected and the teacups she'd inherited from her grandmother.

She also needed to run to the store to stock up on everyday necessities for the pantry and laundry-room cupboards, but that wouldn't take long. As to when she would feel like she truly belonged in the town house, Emily couldn't begin to come up with a timeline.

"Is there anything else we can help with?" one of the delivery guys asked.

Emily hesitated. They had done all she'd asked and more, but once they left, she'd be alone in her own house for the first time. *But that's why you moved out,* she reminded herself. *To be on your own.*

Taking a breath, she offered the young men a smile as she walked to the door. "Thank you for all your help. You've done a great job. I appreciate all the hard work."

The kids' eyes lit up as she handed them a substantial tip.

Tucking the money into their back pockets as they stepped outside, one of them said, "Hey, thanks. If you need anything else, give us a call."

Whatever Emily might have said froze in her throat, despite the burst of desert-dry heat outside. Dressed in blue jeans and a black T-shirt, his dark gaze hidden by a pair of sunglasses, Javy was walking up the driveway. The second she saw him again, Emily knew any time she'd spent in the past few days thinking she might push the man from her mind had clearly been wasted.

He didn't simply fill her thoughts; he filled her senses. She drank in the sight of him—his thick hair, combed back from the sculpted plane of his face, his broad shoulders, the long-legged stride carrying him nearer. Nothing escaped her notice, not the frown the sunglasses couldn't hide or the nicks and cuts on his hands—proof of the hard work he'd been putting in at the restaurant.

"Hey." His deep voice sent a shiver down her spine as he drew close enough for her to catch the clean scent of soap, aftershave and a hint of fabric softener, which had her longing to bury her face against the soft cotton stretching across his broad chest….

"Thanks again," the delivery guy said as he and his co-worker skirted around Javy on their way to the truck.

For a moment, the loud roar and the diesel smell of the engine rumbled through the air. The sound gradually faded away, leaving behind a silence filled with energy every bit as restrained.

"Anna told me you've already moved in," Javy said finally, his tone almost accusing.

"I had some of my things brought over and had the furniture delivered."

"You could have called me," he said.

"You were busy," Emily countered, feeling a flicker of anger.

Had he expected her to put her plans on hold just so she could wait for the off chance he might be free? Or did he, like her parents, think she was making a mistake by rushing into this decision?

Frustration written in his movements, Javy stripped off the sunglasses. Emily thought she was prepared, but the sight of his dark-lashed espresso eyes stole her breath all over again.

"I'm sorry. I was—" Javy began but stopped short.

His frown faded as he reached out and brushed a wayward curl back from her cheek, reminding Emily that her hair was gathered in a ponytail, her face was scrubbed free of makeup, and she was wearing a tank top and a pair of stretch pants. It was not how she wanted to look the first time she saw him after their failed date.

"I'm here now. And I'd like to see what you've done with the place," he added.

Emily wanted to say no. The house wasn't ready for guests, and she wasn't ready for Javy. Even though she hadn't seen him in days, she needed more time to get accustomed to the idea that Javy had been in love once, engaged to a woman who broke his heart and that he might love her still.

She figured it might take years to reconcile a heartbroken Javy with the carefree flirt she'd come to know, but she didn't have years. If the last few days were anything to go by, Javy was already inching toward the end, letting her down easy before he dropped her altogether. If she were smart, *she'd* make the break and protect herself.

But he was here now. Right in front of her, close enough to touch, and she couldn't let him go.

"Come in," she whispered, opening the door to her home, very much aware of how close she was to letting him into her heart.

He folded up his sunglasses and tucked them into the collar of his T-shirt before crossing the threshold. Emily closed the door, feeling oddly nervous as he scanned the great room and kitchen beyond. After all her years surrounded by her parents' formal furniture, Emily had purposely chosen more casual, comfortable pieces with an almost country feel, thanks to the light oak wood and floral and gingham patterns.

"Emily," he said finally, "the place looks great. You did an amazing job."

Dropping onto the couch, she hugged a green-and-white-checked pillow to her chest. "I went shopping. The delivery guys did the rest."

"Don't."

She let her gaze rise to meet his, surprised by the almost rough command behind the one word. He lowered his lean body onto the couch, beside her, with enough deliberation for Emily to feel like prey stalked by a dangerous, gorgeous animal.

Angling toward her, he pulled away the pillow, which would have made a poor shield had she been looking for some kind of defense. But Emily didn't think there was any protection against the weakness that attacked from the inside out. Her bones seemed to melt from the heat of his muscled thigh pressed alongside hers.

"Don't minimize what you've done here. The place looks great. It looks…" His gaze swept the room, as if he were searching for the perfect word amid the entertainment center, coffee table or matching peach-and-green floral wingback chairs flanking the window. Finally, his dark gaze came back to her. "It looks like you."

Grasping at his words as a reprieve from the masculine temptation sharing her couch cushion, Emily looked around the great room. She thought of her place as comfortable, casual, and she couldn't think of a higher compliment. "Thank you. I love it already," she said, ignoring the uncertainty that had plagued her only moments before.

A completely different flurry of nerves took flight when she noticed that Javy's focus had dropped to her mouth. As if he'd flipped a switch in her mind, memories of his kiss replayed with HD clarity.

If this was his way of breaking up with her, she *really* couldn't read men at all.

"Javy—"

"We finished the restaurant this morning," he interrupted, as if sensing she'd been on the verge of asking a "where is this going" type question. "All we have to do tomorrow is touch up some of the paint, do a final cleanup and move the tables and chairs back in."

"That's great. You finished with a whole day to spare."

"Yeah, and well, with the extra night before the reopening, we're having a get-together tomorrow. Just friends and family for chips and salsa and the best margaritas you've ever tasted. I'd like you to be there with me."

Faint hesitation colored the edges of his normally confident smile, and the sight of that unexpected vulnerability went to her head—and her heart—in a way tequila never could.

He still wanted to see her. Had she overreacted to his absence the last few days? Was being busy a legitimate reason and not a lame excuse? With hope spinning through her system like a good buzz, she spoke without thinking. "I'd love to. I can't wait to see the restaurant now that it's complete." When she realized a second later what day tomorrow was, disappointment crashed down on her. "But I can't."

"You can't?"

Emily shook her head. "I totally forgot. I'm helping my mother with a dinner party tomorrow night. I promised I'd be there. My father is offering a partnership to one of his employees. The dinner is sort of a welcome to the family." When Javy's eyebrows lowered, Emily hurried to explain. "The family business, I mean. Not…anything else."

Her explanation doing little to dispel his scowl, he demanded, "Tell me something, Emily. Did your father plan to offer Todd that same position?"

Seeing where Javy was going—and perhaps even where her *mother* was going with the dinner party—Emily reluctantly confessed, "Yes, he did. But obviously his plans changed."

"Have they?"

"Yes." She shot to her feet, wishing he hadn't taken the pillow from her, so she could hit him with it. "I'm not going to suddenly decide Dan Rogers is perfect for me just because my parents like him. Although I'm not sure it's any of your business who I date. I mean, this is all just for fun, right? Nothing serious, nothing lasting. Why would you even care if my parents did roll me out like some kind of welcome mat?"

"I would care," Javy ground out. His eyes had darkened to onyx with each word she spoke. He slowly pushed himself up from the couch, energy and anger barely restrained in each deliberate move. If she had felt stalked before, now she was staring at the predator seconds before he pounced.

"Why?" Emily demanded.

"Because," he said as he reached out. "Because of this."

His hands closed over her arms and dragged her up against his chest. His mouth slammed over hers, and she tasted his jealousy, his anger, but beneath the masculine display of force, she tasted the passion he'd stomped out the night in his kitchen.

Some purely feminine instinct stilled her every response— *her* jealousy, *her* anger, *her* passion. And she waited. For his kiss to soften, for his touch to gentle. Gradually, his hands eased around her back, and his kiss whispered against her lips in an apology. Only then did Emily wrap her arms around his waist and kiss him in return.

But if she'd been waiting for his kiss to ask rather than demand, it seemed Javy had been waiting for her to answer. As soon as she did, he pulled back, even though she didn't want him to go…even though she never wanted him to go.

"Javy—"

"I would care," he repeated, picking up the conversation where he'd left off, though his voice now had a husky, hoarse edge, thanks to the breath-stealing, soul-stealing kiss. "Because the thought of you with another guy drives me crazy."

He backed away then, his gaze never letting go of hers as he walked to the door and left as quickly as he'd arrived. Only after he was gone did Emily wonder what Javy would say if he knew the truth. If he knew she'd never been with anyone. Not with Connor. Not with Todd. Not with any of the other guys she'd dated to make her parents happy.

To a man with Javy's experience, she figured it would be the one thing guaranteed to send him running without a single look back.

Emily had expected her first night in her new house to be somewhat restless. After all, she was sleeping in a new bed, in a new place, with all kinds of new sounds to get used to.

What she had not expected was to toss and turn most of the night, reliving Javy's every kiss, every touch. She'd wanted him to stay, wanted him in a way she'd never wanted another man—with her whole heart and her whole body.

But while she knew he would take very, very good care of her body, she didn't know if she could trust him with her heart. The last few days had shown her how easily, how quickly Javy could disappear from her life.

She wasn't so naive as to think making love would keep

him around, and despite her longing to have him stay the night before, she feared it would only be that much harder to let him go.

The mostly sleepless night did not put her in the best state of mind for Dan Rogers's dinner party, but man-induced insomnia wasn't exactly the kind of thing that would work as an excuse with her mother.

Walking up to the front door of her parents' house, she hesitated briefly. The home where she'd grown up was no longer hers, but did that mean she was supposed to ring the doorbell like some stranger? She certainly hoped her parents wouldn't simply barge into her house, but it seemed like knocking would only emphasize the uncomfortable distance that already existed between her and her parents right then.

Making up her mind, Emily gave a quick knock before unlocking the door. She realized soon enough that it was a good thing she hadn't expected anyone to let her in. No one was around. The family room and her father's study were empty, and only when she made her way to the back of the house and the kitchen did she hear voices.

Charlene had gone with Emily's suggestion of hiring a personal chef to cook the night's meal, and the chef had also arranged for a server. As Emily pushed open the swinging door, the two women were hard at work. She watched as they feinted and dodged each other, despite the spaciousness of the kitchen, checking on pans in the oven, pots on the stove and an array of vegetables readied for salads. The chef lifted a lid, setting free a burst of steam and the delicious scent of lobster bisque, which wafted through the kitchen.

Overseeing every movement in the kitchen like a general prepping for attack, Charlene's eagle-eyed attention broke for a second as she glanced at Emily. If she'd had any doubt about the importance Charlene was placing on that night's dinner, her outfit would have spelled it out. The ice-blue pantsuit her mother wore was new, and an heirloom necklace decorated her throat—a strand of pearls brought from the safe only on special occasions.

Emily was to have worn them on her wedding day.

"Emily, I'm glad you're here. If you could check the dining room one more time before everyone arrives…"

Nodding, Emily gladly made her escape and headed toward the other room. She stopped short in the doorway. The room looked the same as always—narrow floor-to-ceiling windows overlooking the backyard and pool, off-white wainscot giving way to gold-and-cream-striped wallpaper, and crystal chandelier hanging over a table large enough to seat twenty—except the table's massive leaves had been removed, and the table was set for a cozy gathering of six.

"How does everything look?" Charlene asked a few minutes later as she entered the room.

"How does it look?" Emily echoed, realizing she'd been set up. "I'd say it looks a little small. Where are the settings for the other guests?"

"What do you mean?" Charlene asked, averting her gaze to adjust a perfectly straight linen napkin.

"You told me we were having six guests."

Her mother waved a hand. "And the table is set for six."

"So that's you, Daddy, Aileen, her husband, me…and Dan Rogers. That's *one* guest, Mother, not six."

Charlene sighed. "I kept the dinner party to family to give you and Dan a chance to get to know one another." Her mother's gaze pleaded with her to step back in line, to do what was expected, to make *everyone* happy. "Dan is intelligent, educated. He's been with your father's company for years."

"All of which makes him a perfect candidate to become Daddy's partner but—"

"He's also single. He broke up with his long-term girlfriend a few months ago."

Crossing her arms over the twisted feeling in her stomach, Emily whispered, "Javy was right."

"What does he have to do with this?"

Emily shook her head. "Nothing."

The doorbell rang, and Charlene glanced toward the sound before looking back at her daughter, anticipation clearly written in her eyes.

Feeling bruised and battered from banging her head against a brick wall, Emily said, "I'll get it."

As she walked down the hallway to the foyer, she knew she'd told her mother the truth. This wasn't about Javy being right. This was about her. Despite buying her own house and moving in, she hadn't changed as much as she liked to believe. She was still the same old Emily, faking a smile and doing what would make her parents happy, instead of following her own dreams.

Chapter Twelve

"Leave for a week, and see how things change."

Though the pre-reopening was for friends and family only, the restaurant was nearly packed, but Javy recognized the familiar drawl above the mix of music, laughter and non-stop talking.

After setting a tray of guacamole, sour cream and salsa on a table already crowded with chips, *taquitos* and mini chimichangas, Javy turned to face Connor McClane. Connor stood in the middle of the restaurant, a pair of sunglasses pushed to the top of his head, tanned skin and wide smile signs of his recent return from his Hawaiian honeymoon.

"When did you get back?" Javy asked, slapping his friend on the back.

"Just this morning." Connor took a look around and asked, "Been busy while I was gone?"

"Yeah. You?" Javy asked drily.

Connor's smile broadened, boasting his happiness with the woman he loved. "We had a blast," he said. His expression quickly faded. "You could have told me about the restaurant."

Javy sighed. "The pipe broke during your wedding, hours before you were leaving town. There wasn't anything you could do."

"I would have helped," Connor insisted.

"I didn't need your help. Not this time." Realizing how his words sounded when he should have been…when he *was* grateful for Connor's help, Javy added, "Alex and his crew did most of the work, and the insurance money will cover the damage this time."

"Good. I'm glad." Connor paused before adding, "I hear the restaurant isn't the only change going on around here."

"Been talking to the in-laws?"

"Yeah, I spoke with Gordon. He said you paid him back the ten thousand dollars."

Javy snorted. "Did he tell you he returned the check?"

"No. Did he?"

"Yep. Got it in the mail this morning."

Javy grabbed a beer from a huge galvanized tub and twisted off the top as if wringing someone's smug neck. He passed the bottle to Connor before going back for number two. Javy had been furious when he opened the envelope that morning, especially following his argument with Emily the night before, but he couldn't disguise a touch of respect for the older man.

"Doesn't matter, though. I'm not staying away from Emily," he added.

And he sure as hell wasn't going to admit that right now Emily was staying away from him. Having dinner with her family and their newest selection of socially perfect boyfriends. Emily might have thought it was a simple family dinner, but Javy could read between the lines of her parents' matchmaking.

Gordon Wilson had found someone he trusted enough to hand over partial control of his company. If the guy was that smart, that educated, and good-looking to boot, why wouldn't the Wilsons want Emily to go out with him?

"The family's just worried about Emily," Connor said.

"Emily can take care of herself. It's what she's wanted all along, but no one's given her the chance."

Including me, Javy realized suddenly. He hadn't really taken her decision to move out seriously, at least not as a long-term commitment, until he saw the house the day before. In a matter of days, she'd turned the place into a real home, not just some temporary abode to see how the other half lived.

"If it isn't my beautiful bride," Connor said as Kelsey's arrival broke into Javy's thoughts. He watched his friend pull his new wife into his arms. "I missed you."

Laughter bubbled out of Kelsey, her brown eyes sparkling. "I was gone all of five minutes while I talked to Maria."

"Like I said, I missed you," Connor told her.

Kelsey rolled her eyes, but a blush of pleasure lit her freckled cheeks. "Can you believe this guy?" she asked.

The question was rhetorical, but Javy was starting to believe. To believe that Connor and Kelsey had found the real thing. To believe maybe he and Emily could have it, too.

Connor smiled. "That reminds me. I better go say hi to your mother. I'll be right back."

Once Connor excused himself, Kelsey turned her speculative gaze on Javy, showing him how the five-foot-nothing redhead had given his friend a run for his money before they tied the knot. He also had a good idea exactly what Kelsey and his mother had talked about.

He could have come up with an excuse and made his escape, but Kelsey was Emily's cousin….

"Did you know your uncle's offering a partnership to one of his employees?" Javy asked.

Kelsey's eyebrows rose, her surprise evident, but her response was 100 percent Wilson composure. "I did."

"So tell me about this guy."

"Why?" she asked, but this time the surprise was completely absent. "Are you that interested in my uncle's company?"

He didn't give a damn about Gordon Wilson's company, except when it came to Emily. "I'm interested if the Wilsons think the guy is as perfect for the family as he is for the family business."

"Javy—"

"You've met him, right?" he asked, pressing.

"Yes, Dan Rogers has stopped by the house a few times to meet with my uncle. He's always seemed like a nice guy. He had a steady girlfriend up until a few months ago, but evidently that's changed."

"Evidently," he bit out. When Kelsey didn't reply, staring at him like he'd sprouted a third eye, he demanded, "What?"

Kelsey leaned closer, sympathy filling her expression. "We've all been wrong. We've been worried about Emily getting hurt, but her heart isn't the one at risk of getting broken. Is it, Javy?"

Whatever denial he might have made stuck in his throat when a flash of blond hair across the room stole his attention. He did a double take as he caught sight of Emily making her way through the restaurant. He might have thought his mind was playing tricks on him, but his imagination had nothing on the real woman.

She looked amazing in a black-and-white print dress with a flared skirt that emphasized her small waist and long legs. A black headband held back her blond hair, showing off her flawless skin, wide blue eyes and elegant features. Her smile lit the room as she stopped to talk to Anna.

Vaguely aware of Kelsey taking the beer bottle from his hand, Javy thought he heard her say, "Tell her how you feel."

Or maybe that was his own conscience advising him after failing miserably last night to keep his mouth shut.

He crossed the new tile floor to reach her, and everyone in the restaurant faded away as Emily met his gaze. A touch of color brightened her cheeks as he caught her hand and pulled her away from his cousin in midsentence. Finding a less crowded corner near the hallway to the kitchen, he leaned close enough to talk quietly. Close enough to catch the scent of her perfume. Close enough to see the pulse jump at the base of her throat. But *not* close enough to taste that spot of silky skin no matter how badly he wanted to…

"I didn't expect to see you here," he murmured.

"I know. I'm sorry."

"No. Don't apologize. I'm just glad you're here now." His gaze traveled over her from head to toe. "You look…amazing."

Jealousy surged inside him—he knew that she'd gotten dressed up for another man—but he shoved the emotion aside. It didn't matter who she'd been with earlier; all he cared about was that she was here with him now.

"I left as soon as I could," Emily was saying. "But I had to stay for a while. I'd promised my mother."

"I know." He knew about familial commitments and obligations better than anyone. "I had no right to react the way I did last night."

The possessiveness he felt was as foreign as his earlier jealousy, especially since he had no claim on Emily. None but the one his heart had made.

"It's okay."

"No, it isn't," he insisted.

She'd been right when she said her personal life was none of his business. But he wanted it to be. For the first time in years, he wanted more than fun, more than casual. But that street went both ways. If he expected Emily to tell him everything, he would have to do the same. Starting with Stephanie and the conversation he'd avoided that night at his house.

"You were right, you know," Emily said. "My parents, at least my mother, was hoping to welcome Dan Rogers to more than the business."

Dan had been everything her mother had promised: smart, educated, charming and handsome. He even possessed a sense of humor, which might have made the dinner party enjoyable if her every thought hadn't centered around *this* party.

Emily never would have thought she'd have a reason to thank Todd, but their failed engagement had definitely shown her that something had been missing from the relationship. And thanks to Javy, she now knew what that something was. That instant rush of attraction, the longing to be with him, to talk with him, to laugh with him, to love him, grew deeper and deeper every day....

It was something she certainly hadn't experienced with Todd or with Dan Rogers. She'd never experienced it with any man but Javy, and she doubted she ever would again. And though the moment wasn't meant to last, it was one she fully intended to enjoy here and now.

Staring up at the planes and angles of his handsome face, she announced, "But I don't want Dan Rogers, Javy."

His dark gaze scoured her features, and Emily feared how much she'd revealed. "Emily—"

"A toast!" an exuberant voice called out, breaking the moment. "To the newlyweds."

A cheer went up from the two dozen or so people gathered in the dining area, and Emily caught sight of Kelsey and Connor in the crowd. "Is that... I didn't realize they were back from their honeymoon."

"They got back this morning. I wasn't sure they'd make it."

As Emily watched, Connor took Kelsey's margarita from her hand, set the glass aside and pulled her into his arms for a kiss, which drew catcalls from the crowd.

A kiss filled with so much love and tenderness, a shaft of longing pierced Emily's heart.

"You okay?" Javy murmured.

Embarrassed he might have seen that longing written on her face, Emily immediately said, "I'm fine. I…" The speculation in his gaze sunk in, and she realized he'd misread whatever he might have seen. "I couldn't be happier for Kelsey. Connor's a great guy, and he's been a good friend, but whatever we had in the past is just that—in the past."

Javy nodded, but Emily wasn't convinced. Maybe because *his* past—a past he refused to talk about—was still so much a part of his present.

A few hours later Emily didn't have a single doubt that the reopening would be a huge success, judging by that evening's party atmosphere. Laughter nearly drowned out the music playing in the background, and dozens of conversations were going on at one time.

Stories and pictures of Kelsey and Connor's wedding and honeymoon were passed around, details about the damage done to the restaurant were shared and tours were given to show off the work Alex and Javy had done.

Emily loved the tile in the hallway to the bathrooms. Cream-colored tiles lined the walls, interspersed with hand-painted pieces in greens, blues and reds. The color scheme continued into the bathrooms, where the decorative tiles lined the mirrors and accented the countertops.

Everyone commented about the amazing job, and while Alex soaked up the praise, Javy took it all in stride, and Emily wondered if he didn't see the job as incomplete, with the patio and bar area untouched.

Needing a break, Emily slipped away from the party and stepped out onto the patio, willing to brave the hot, stifling night for a few seconds of quiet. A slight breeze made the heat bearable and set the branches of bougainvillea, with their fuchsia blooms, waving.

The sliding-glass doors muffled the sounds of the party inside, and only a muted light spilled out onto the brick patio, scarcely chasing shadows into the corners.

Emily jumped when a sudden movement caught her eye.

Maria Delgado pushed out of a chair on the far side of the patio.

"I'm sorry, Mrs. Delgado. I didn't realize anyone was out here. I'll go back—"

"Wait a moment, Emily," Javy's mother said. "We should talk."

"All right," Emily agreed, hoping Maria didn't hear the reluctance in her voice.

When the older woman sat back down, Emily crossed the patio to join her. Despite her proclamation, Maria didn't say anything, a burst of laughter coming from inside the restaurant emphasizing the silence.

"The restaurant looks amazing," Emily said finally, picking a subject obviously close to the woman's heart. "Javy worked so hard to have everything back the way it was before the water damage. You should be proud of him."

Maria's shoulders drew back. "He is my son. Of course, I am proud of him."

"No, I didn't mean…" With a sound of frustration, Emily let her explanation die. Somehow she'd gotten off on the wrong foot with Maria Delgado, and she doubted anything would change that.

She was searching for an excuse to make her way back inside when Maria said, "You are doing a good thing, donating your clothes, helping with Angela's charity."

A polite response formed in Emily's thoughts, even though she knew Maria didn't mean the words as a compliment. Unwilling to simply smile and let it go, she said, "And yet you don't sound impressed."

"Is that why you do this? To impress me?"

"Of course not."

"Ah." Maria nodded. "To impress my son."

"No, that's not it, either," Emily argued, the first flicker of anger sparking inside her. "I'm doing this because I want to help. Because I know how lucky I am, how blessed I've been my entire life." A point that talking to Lauren had certainly driven home. "I want to do what I can to give something back. And if you don't believe that… Well, there's nothing I can do about it."

Maria sighed. "I do believe you, Emily. You're a nice girl. A pretty girl. But you aren't the girl who will make my Javy settle down."

At the older woman's words, a knot twisted in Emily's stomach, even though she had known going in that any relationship with Javier Delgado was not meant to last. She certainly wasn't foolish enough to think *she* would be the woman to change his playboy ways.

And that was what she should have told his mother, but when she opened her mouth, a completely unexpected question came out. "Because I'm not like Stephanie?"

She couldn't deny her curiosity about the woman Javy had once been engaged to, a woman who had once settled Javy down.

Even in the faint lighting, Emily saw Maria's eyes widen. "My son told you about her?"

Javy hadn't told her much, and Emily suddenly regretted asking. If he'd wanted her to know, *he* would have told her. His refusal was a reminder that she shouldn't let herself get too close, a reminder Emily feared she had ignored.

Shaking her head, Emily pushed out of the chair. "It doesn't matter. I should go back."

Maria caught her arm before she could leave. "It is not because you are different from Stephanie that I worry," she said, a hint of sorrow pulling at her features. "It is because you are too much the same."

The same? She and Javy's ex-fiancée were somehow alike? The questions swirled through Emily's thoughts, but when Maria's fingers slipped away with the faint jingle of bracelets at her wrist, Emily backed toward the sliding-glass doors. If Javy didn't want to tell her about Stephanie, she wasn't going to ask.

And while she might not know much of anything about Javy's past, she *did* know him. Well enough to point out to Maria, "You should have let Javy remodel the patio and the bar. It would have meant a lot to him, more than you seem to know."

At the end of the evening any number of people could have driven Javy home. He was pretty sure he could have managed it himself. After his first beer, he'd switched to margaritas, but with Alex behind the bar, guaranteeing the drinks were more tequila than lime, Javy didn't want to risk it.

So, without any real planning on either of their parts, amid hugs of farewell and high fives, he and Emily drifted toward her car.

She filled the ride with idle small talk, mostly about the restaurant and the following night's reopening. "It will be a huge success, just like tonight. I'm glad I could come."

"So am I."

"I had a really good time."

"Despite what my mother said to you?" he drawled.

Emily's gaze cut to his before refocusing on the road ahead. The passing streetlights flashed over her profile like the flickering of a black-and-white television set. "How did you—"

"I saw you come in from the patio, and I know my mother was already outside."

He doubted Maria had missed the chance to say something to Emily about their relationship. His mother had been bemoaning his single status for years. It was one of the reasons he usually kept the women he dated far, far away from Maria.

The last thing he'd needed was his mother putting ideas in anyone's head. Until now. Until Emily. He wouldn't mind so much if his mother put some of those ideas into *her* head.

"It doesn't matter," she said finally.

"Emily—"

"It's not important, Javy," she insisted. "Really."

And maybe that was part of the problem. He wanted their relationship to matter. He wanted it to be important, life altering. He wanted their relationship to be forever. That realization had his stomach churning, as if he'd had a dozen or so margaritas, instead of two or three.

"I think," he said, actually *hoping,* "it might be important."

But despite the opening he gave her, Emily didn't speak for the rest of the ride.

Javy waited until they arrived at his place and he invited Emily inside before pressing the point. "What did my mother say to you?"

Seated on his couch, which was definitely built more for comfort than style, Emily maintained perfect posture. She smoothed the skirt of her dress over her knees. "She's your mother. She wants you to be happy."

"And?"

"She wants to see you settle down." Nothing Emily said

came as a surprise until she added, "She doesn't think it's going to happen."

"She doesn't?" His mother was giving up on him? That didn't sound like Maria at all. And wouldn't that be ironic? For her to give up on the idea of him settling down just as he found the one woman he wanted to get serious about.

"I thought maybe it had to do with Stephanie." Emily turned to face him on the couch, drawing up one knee and distracting him with her bare skin and a toned, shapely calf. "I shouldn't have brought it up, and your mother really didn't tell me anything, but I want to apologize for going behind your back. It wasn't right and—"

"And you shouldn't have had to do it," Javy interrupted. "I should have told you."

"You don't have to…."

"I want to," he insisted. "Stephanie was my first serious girlfriend. We dated at the end of our senior year in high school. We thought…*I* thought we were in love," he amended, since to this day he still wasn't sure if Stephanie had loved him or had simply seen him as a ticket to freedom.

"What was she like?" Emily asked.

He expected a certain amount of curiosity; he would have felt the same had he not already heard so much about Emily's ex. But something more—a reluctance—was hidden behind the question.

Maybe she's afraid you're gonna act like a jerk and cut her off the way you did last time she asked, his conscience goaded.

Hoping to wipe the hesitancy from her eyes, he insisted, "You can ask me anything you want, Emily."

She nodded, but the worry didn't entirely disappear.

Determined to tell her everything, he said, "Stephanie was beautiful. She looked… Well, I guess she looked a little like you. She was blonde and had blue eyes." But that was where the similarities ended, and maybe that was why he'd never paid much attention to the likeness before. "Stephanie was troubled and...fragile."

"Fragile? How?" With Emily's focus locked on the floral pattern of her skirt, Javy couldn't see her expression, but he could almost sense her frown.

"Her parents divorced when she was eleven, and they spent the next several years bouncing from one family court to another, fighting over custody of her. She felt like a pawn, and for as long as I knew her, all she talked about was the day she could finally escape."

He should have realized that he was little more than a ticket out of town. At eighteen, he, too, had had big plans of striking out on his own, not because he'd had a bad home life, but simply because, well, hell, he'd been eighteen. He'd thought he knew it all and was ready to see it all, do it all. When Stephanie agreed to his every suggestion, he'd believed it was because she loved him and wanted to be with him, no matter what the adventure.

Too late had he realized all she wanted was the getaway car; it didn't really matter who was driving.

He went on. "I proposed the night of our graduation. It seemed like the perfect time. We were riding high on success, and nothing could stop us. Or at least that's what I thought."

"What happened?"

"I told my parents our plans, and my dad flipped out. I'd never seen him so angry. Everything we said to each other built this wall of anger and bitterness until, finally, neither one of us could get through to the other. And then...my dad had a heart attack. It was only a few weeks after our fight. The doctors said stress might have been the cause...."

"Oh, Javy."

Reaching out, Emily took his hands in hers and let her

touch convey all she couldn't say. Her presence, her compassion, did more to sooth his guilt than any words ever could.

"I thought graduating from high school and getting engaged meant I was an adult. I found out real fast what growing up really meant. My mother was at my dad's side twenty-four-seven, and that put me in charge at the restaurant. I had spent my whole life around that place and had worked there since I was in junior high, but running it—that was completely different. I couldn't just be one of the guys anymore. I was the boss, whether they liked it or not. Whether *I* liked it or not."

Overnight he'd had responsibility thrust on him, and he could now admit, in some ways he'd been running from it ever since.

"I told Stephanie I couldn't leave as long as my dad was in the hospital. I still wanted to get married, just not as soon as we'd planned. I expected her to understand and fooled myself into thinking she did."

"What happened?"

"My dad never left the hospital. The doctors thought he was improving, but he had a second heart attack and…" He swallowed hard, the memories still raw after all these years. Regret clawed at him for the fight they'd had and the missed chance of ever making amends. "After that, there was no way I could leave town with Stephanie. But we could still get married, find an apartment near the restaurant, start our life together."

Looking back now, Javy didn't know how he'd thought their marriage could work. His father had been right when he'd called him selfish and irresponsible. He and Stephanie had been self-centered kids, focused only on what they wanted. And while tragedy had forced a change in his plans, Stephanie's plans had remained the same.

He continued. "I tried spending as much time as I could with her, but my mother was in no shape to be running the restaurant. Sometimes I felt like I lived there, so I don't suppose

I can blame Stephanie for feeling abandoned. And then, one day, I found a note stuck on the windshield of my car."

Emily squeezed his hand. "I'm so sorry."

He waited for the dark memories to sweep over him like a summer monsoon, filled with flashes of anger and earsplitting roars of protest, but like a storm that dissipated over the desert, all he felt was the faint brush of relief.

"I couldn't go after her. Couldn't just take off after I'd promised my mother that I could handle running the restaurant and that she didn't have to worry about a thing. And then there was the fire."

Even after ten years, guilt sliced through his gut with the memory. As the manager, it had been his job to do a final walk-through of the restaurant each night. To this day, he would swear he'd checked the stoves before leaving that night. But exhaustion and constant worry had taken a toll, and while he'd been so *sure,* he'd also been so wrong.

"We were at home when we got the phone call from the fire department." He would never forget the look in his mother's eyes—not a look of anger or devastation, which he could have handled, but a look of utter defeat. He'd seen a woman who simply had nothing left to lose. "It was my fault."

"No," Emily protested.

"I should have checked the kitchen one more time."

Emily shifted closer, bracing one hand on his shoulder and curving her fingers around his jaw to turn his face toward her. "That doesn't make it your fault. It was an accident. You said your mother wasn't in any shape to run the restaurant. But what kind of shape were you in?"

He'd been a mess. His father's death and Stephanie's desertion had hit him hard. Add the responsibility of managing the restaurant on top of that, and it was little surprise that something had to give. But for it to be his family's restaurant…

"It was not your fault," Emily insisted. "You need to stop blaming yourself. To let go and move on." Javy opened his mouth to argue, but she beat him to it. "Why didn't you push harder to remodel the restaurant?"

"It's like you said. My mother wants to keep everything as it was when my father was still alive."

"Is that the reason? Or is it because you think she won't trust your ideas? Because *you* don't trust those ideas?"

He didn't like the thought that he'd let failure control his life, but he had. Between the fire at the restaurant and Stephanie's desertion, he'd changed. Oh, he'd told himself and everyone else that all he wanted out of life was to have some fun and enjoy his freedom, but he'd lied. He wasn't having fun, and he wasn't free. He was afraid and running scared.

But as he gazed into Emily's eyes—at the understanding, the concern, the confidence he saw there—everything inside him slowed, stilled and stopped.

He didn't have to run anymore. Not when he'd finally found the one place he wanted to be and the one person he wanted to be with.

Chapter Thirteen

With Javy staring at her so intently, Emily wondered if she'd pushed too far. If like the night of their date, she was going to ruin a wonderful evening by asking too many questions.

Her stomach twisted at the idea of Javy pulling away from her again, but it was a risk she had to take. She couldn't go back to trying to make everyone else happy by keeping her mouth shut with a smile.

Not even for Javy. Especially not for Javy.

"You know the changes will only make the restaurant that much better, and you deserve the chance to prove it to yourself and to Maria," she said.

"I know."

"And the only way to do that is to talk to her again, to try and make her see…" So caught up in her own argument, she didn't even realize she'd won. "You what?"

He chuckled at her confusion. "There is such a thing as quitting while you're ahead, sweetheart."

"I'm not sure I've ever been ahead before. I didn't realize I was there."

All teasing aside, she drew her right leg up onto the couch. Javy caught her around the waist, steadying her, as she cupped his face in her hands. His evening beard scraped against her palms, a rough contrast as she ran her thumb over his lips.

"I think…" Emily felt the brush of breath and movement against her flesh as he spoke, and a shiver raced from her fingertips up her arm to scatter goose bumps across her chest. "I think there's a way for both of us to get what we want. For my mother to keep the restaurant and her memories intact, and for me to get what I want, too."

"How?"

"I'll tell you," he promised, "but first I need some time to work out the details. And second, I don't want to talk about the restaurant or my mother or my past anymore tonight."

Sliding her fingers back into the soft hair at the nape of his neck, she tilted her head to the side. "Hmm. What do you want to talk about?"

Judging by the heat in his eyes as his gaze dropped to her lips, she expected him to say he didn't want to talk at all. But he surprised her, answering, "Let's talk about you."

"Me? I think we've already determined that you know everything about me."

"Not…everything." His gaze dropped from her eyes to her lips to her breasts, sending flames of heat licking over her body. And despite his earlier words, she didn't think talking was what he had in mind.

But it was enough to remind her of the one thing about her she still hadn't mentioned. Emily opened her mouth, but she still couldn't bring herself to blurt out the truth. And when

Javy did as he'd suggested and started talking about her, a single sentence or coherent thought was nowhere to be found.

His words, his voice, his lips poured over her. Emily had heard compliments before, but never murmured so intimately against her skin and never spoken in Spanish. A bubble of giddy laughter broke from her lips, despite the hand she instantly slapped over her mouth.

Javy gazed at her, a question in his eyes, but confidence in his smile. "Should I even ask?"

"I was—" another giggle interrupted "—just thinking my father was right."

His dark brow slammed down in a frown. "Your father?"

Emily nodded, fisting his shirt in one hand as she pulled him close again. "Spanish is, oh, so practical."

His lips kicked up in a smile. "Ah, the benefits of a prep-school education. Tell me, Miss Wilson, what else did you learn?"

Not nearly as much as he could teach her, Emily thought as he eased her back against the couch pillows. She sank into the softness, a definite contrast to the strength and hardness of his body as he followed her down. He claimed her lips again even as his fingers drifted toward the buttons on her dress. Could he feel the way her heart was about to pound out of her chest?

As his hand closed over her breast, she forgot to care. The pleasure of his touch burned all nerves, all hesitation, even embarrassment. If only it would burn away the satin and lace of her bra, so she could feel the heat of his flesh against her own. Then suddenly the barrier was gone, brushed aside by impatient hands or reduced to ash, Emily didn't know. She could barely focus on anything beyond the play of his fingers against her breast and the desire he drew from an endless well inside of her.

But despite the pleasure of his touch, Emily needed more. She needed to know, to see, to *feel* that Javy wanted her as much as she wanted him. With his experience, of course, he could turn her on. But she needed to know she could do the same, had to believe this meant *something* to Javy beyond the usual seduction....

Following his lead, she held his gaze as her fingers found the buttons on his shirt and slowly slid each one free. His skin was hot and smooth against her palms, and she couldn't get enough, not only of touching him, but of his reaction. The way his eyes darkened, the way his breath caught and his pulse pounded, the way his stomach muscles clenched as her fingers drifted lower.

If she had any questions about the intensity of Javy's response, she had her answer when he caught her mouth in a kiss that seared away any doubts. His kiss still held a hint of salt from the margaritas, as well as a taste that was uniquely his own. Emily sought out more of the flavor, rimming his lips the same way the salt had rimmed the glass, until Javy took control, his tongue plunging deep.

Desire curled her hips into his, and reality intruded, whispering through her conscience the words she should have already said before she let things go this far....

When he broke the kiss for a brief moment, she tried to explain. "Javy, I..." Her voice little more than a husky whisper, Emily swallowed and tried again. "You should, um, probably know I've never done this before."

She felt his lips curve into a smile against her neck. "Made love on a couch?"

A nervous laugh bubbled up from inside her. "That, too."

He froze against her, the meaning of her words clearer the second time around. He pulled back with an expression of so much shock, it might have been comical if she hadn't felt so much like crying. "You..."

"I'm sorry." Regret clogged her throat, and she swallowed hard. "I shouldn't have said anything. I didn't want you to stop. I should have—"

"Let your first time take place on the couch in my living room?"

"Yes," she answered, but with enough of a question in her voice to make Javy's head drop to her shoulder in a half laugh, half groan.

"No," he countered, then repeated in a stronger voice, "No." He levered his body off hers, the effort it took obvious in the tension knotting his shoulders and arms. He sank back against the couch cushions, his breathing still ragged and his gaze still touched with disbelief. "Your first time should be special. It should be perfect."

"It would be," she whispered. As long as her first time was with Javy, she knew it would be.

But despite the tension and desire still radiating from every plane and angle of his body, stretched out beside her, Javy shook his head.

She'd feared this would happen. Tears burning her throat, Emily wished she'd kept her mouth shut. She'd known everything would change once she told Javy the truth and that a man of his experience wouldn't be interested in someone with *no* experience.

"How? I mean, you were *engaged*," he pointed out, "and you never—"

"It was a short engagement, and I wanted to wait," she confessed, well aware that if she'd felt for her ex-fiancé one-tenth of what she felt for Javy, she never would have made the suggestion. "Todd agreed easily enough, but of course, his idea of waiting for me meant sleeping with the maid."

An embarrassment she hadn't felt moments earlier now boiled up inside her, heating her face and escaping like steam from every pore. Her fingers trembled on the buttons Javy had slid away so easily. She needed to leave now, before she added to her humiliation by breaking down in tears. She started to push to her feet, but Javy caught her by the wrist.

"What—"

She didn't have the chance to finish her question before he stretched out on the couch and pulled her down beside him. Reaching overhead with his free hand, he clicked off the light. Only a thin square of light outlined the blinds on the front window, and their combined breathing sounded too loud—and too intimate—in the darkness.

He pressed her head to his shoulder. "Close your eyes."

"What—what are you doing?" she demanded, struggling against his hold, still intent on escaping her own inadequacies.

"I'm holding you," he answered, stating the obvious.

"I know, but you don't even want—"

His hoarse laughter cut off the words Emily never meant to say. "Emily, you have no idea…."

"Then why stop?"

"Because you're…and I didn't…" Seeming to have as much trouble explaining his reasoning as Emily was in accepting it, Javy exhaled a sigh, which only settled her closer to him. "I've been imagining making love to you since I saw you at Connor and Kelsey's engagement party," he confessed, his momentary loss for words over. "But I never imagined our first time would be your first time. I want to do this right."

Since it was her first time, Emily thought maybe she should be the one to decide what was right, but at least they would have that time. Relieved her inexperience hadn't completely scared him off, she said, "You're going to hold me while I sleep? All night?"

"Yes."

"But—"

Even in the semidarkness, his fingers unerringly found her lips and silenced her with a touch. "At least there'll be a first for one of us tonight."

Emily smiled as she snuggled next him, resting her head on his chest and her hand on his heart. Because although sleeping in a man's arms would be a first for her, Emily didn't think *she* was the one Javy was talking about.

Emily woke the next morning to sunlight streaming through the living-room blinds. Waking up in an unfamiliar place, still dressed and lying on a couch, she would have expected to suffer a moment or two of disorientation. But she remembered every minute of the previous night up to the moment she fell asleep in Javy's arms.

Now, however, she was alone, battling feelings of disappointment and relief. She would have loved to wake up in his arms, too, but having a few minutes to herself before seeing him again sounded like a good idea. She could wash her face, brush her hair and remind herself that even though she was falling for Javy like a skydiver ready to jump out of a plane without a parachute, nothing—not even last night, as amazing as it had been—said he felt the same.

She was going to hit the ground hard. But until then, Emily thought the best thing she could do was to close her eyes and pretend she could fly.

Sitting up and stretching her arms overhead, she caught sight of a piece of paper on the coffee table, amid a few remote controls and a stack of sports magazines. *Out of coffee. Be back soon. Make yourself at home.*

Emily smiled. Judging by his abbreviated note and slashing cursive, coffee was a must in the morning.

Feeling like a bit of a sneak despite having written permission, she made her way down the hall and peeked into an open doorway. The small guest bath, with its white walls and empty counter, might have lacked extras, but folded on the toilet was a towel, what looked like a pair of navy gym shorts and gray T-shirt, and an unopened toothbrush.

Picking up the small plastic-wrapped box, she pictured a dozen or so stashed away somewhere for morning-after moments exactly like this one, but she thrust the image aside.

"Don't look down," she murmured as she set the toothbrush aside.

Fifteen minutes later, Emily stood on the back patio, clean and refreshed, if not exactly stylish. The intense sunlight, promising another typical hot summer day, blazed down on the lawn, which was lined by citrus trees weighed down with lemons and limes. Around the side of the lot, a structure stood separate from the house. She was wondering what Javy stored inside it when the glass door behind her slid open.

"Hey," he murmured.

Emily turned to face Javy, feeling a little self-conscious when his grin broadened as he took in her bare feet and her arms and legs, left partially exposed by his borrowed—and baggy—clothes. "Morning."

He handed her a cup of coffee from a travel carrier and leaned in for a kiss that packed far more of a punch than caffeine ever could. He tasted like mint toothpaste, and Emily breathed in the scent of soap and shampoo. The longing to wake up every morning with this man hit hard. Her stomach dropped out of her and the ground gave way as she spun into an out-of-control freefall.

Unaware of the panic screaming through her at terminal velocity, Javy stepped back. His gaze roamed over her from her still-damp hair to her bare feet.

"I have always thought everything you wear looks better

on you than it would on anyone else, and this proves it. Those clothes definitely look better on you than they ever did on me."

Thanks to years of practice, Emily managed a smile. "Yes, I'm planning on modeling these when we have the charity fashion show," she said wryly. "I'm sure I'd send the bidding through the roof."

"I can guarantee it, since I would have to outbid everyone there."

"That desperate to get your clothes back, huh?"

"I'm that desperate, all right, but not so much about taking them back as taking them off."

A shiver raced over her skin, reminding Emily how little she wore beneath his clothes. The borrowed shirt was baggy, but the material thin enough to telegraph her reactions. Something she noticed only when his gaze dropped to her breasts.

Just that easily her thoughts were filled with memories of the night before, leaving her feeling weak and ready to pick up where they had left off, with his solid body pressed to hers, his hand at her breast, and nothing to stop them from finishing what they'd started.

But Javy was already dressed for work, and although the reopening party didn't start until that evening, the restaurant was running specials throughout the day. After all the hard work he'd done, he deserved to show it off.

Taking a deep breath, she searched for a distraction other than how gorgeous he looked in the black slacks and crisp white shirt, which so perfectly set off his dark hair and tanned skin. She gestured at the structure she'd noticed earlier and asked, "What do you keep in there?"

"The previous owners had a few ATVs they stored in that garage. I've been using it as sort of a workshop." Javy focused on removing the lid from the coffee cup as he spoke, his words and actions a little too casual for Emily to believe.

"What kind of workshop?"

"Mostly just a place to keep my lawn mower and some tools."

"Uh-huh." If he thought she'd be satisfied with that non-answer, he was mistaken. Backing up, she said, "Maybe I should just go see for myself, since you don't want to tell me."

He caught her arm before she reached the edge of the patio. Even though his grip was light, she felt his muscles tighten, and the tension wiped the teasing smile from her lips.

"Javy, I was only joking."

"I know." He rubbed his thumb along the inside of her elbow.

Was it her imagination, or did that soothing touch actually relax *him?* She brushed the thought aside. It was ridiculous to assume she had that much of an effect on him.

Setting their coffees aside on a small bistro table, he said, "Come on. I'll show you."

Emily couldn't pretend she wasn't curious about what was hidden away in the garage. Obviously more than the vague tools Javy had referred to. But when Javy slid the doors open, she couldn't hide her amazement. "Javy, this is incredible."

Peg-Boards lined all three walls, with more tools hanging side by side in precise alignment than Emily could imagine outside a hardware store. Screwdrivers in ascending size ran right to left. Hammers, saws, pliers, chisels and tools she couldn't name filled every inch of space. A table saw stood in the center of what would normally be a good-sized work space…if not for the tables and chairs crowded around it—tables and chairs Emily recognized.

"The chairs and tables from the restaurant! You refinished them!" she exclaimed.

"Yeah." Javy ran a hand over the carved back of one chair. "The wood was pretty dry, and the water did some serious damage to the legs. I tried to fix them but…"

His voice trailed off, as if he were confessing some undeniable failure, but all Emily saw were the same tables and chairs from the restaurant, with a new, polished finish to the walnut stain. "But what? They look amazing. Like brand-new!"

Javy frowned, as if taking her compliment as criticism. "They're fifteen years old. I wanted them to match—to look the same as all the others. But I don't know. I must have used the wrong kind of varnish. The finish is too high gloss, and it made the stain too dark. I was hoping to have them ready for the reopening, but I'm not going to have time to strip them down again and start over."

"Start over? Don't you dare!" Emily said, dumbfounded that he would even consider scrapping all his hard work. "It doesn't matter if it's not a perfect match or if this isn't how your father would have done it. I know your mother sees changes to the restaurant like she's losing a precious piece of your father. But you aren't taking anything away. You're giving something back. A piece of your dad that Maria has probably already given up as lost and a piece of yourself, as well. How could she not love it?"

And how could *she* not love him? Emily wondered even as she helplessly braced for impact.

Chapter Fourteen

The reopening was in full swing, and the restaurant's usually competent staff was showing signs of nerves. Javy couldn't blame them, even though the excitement charging through his veins had little to do with organizing the additional waiters and waitresses, giving the band he'd hired for the event a hand setting up, or making his way through the dining area to greet the many friends and family who'd stopped by in support.

He was happy with the turnout and hoping for a two-second break to actually enjoy the accomplishment, but his thoughts and, more often than not, his gaze kept drifting toward the front door, searching for Emily. He knew she'd be there; it was impossible to imagine the celebration without her.

It was impossible to imagine his *life* without her.

"So, you're sure it's okay?"

Refocusing on his suddenly uncertain chef, Javy insisted, "It's kick-ass, Juan. Trust me."

The fiftysomething chef had created a new, hotter than hot salsa for the event, to be served with a side of guacamole to cool things off. He'd been messing with the ingredients for the past five minutes, insisting Javy try each adjustment, even though he'd declared the first taste on a crisp tortilla chip perfect.

The cilantro, the heat from half a dozen peppers, and the burst of cool tomato had exploded with flavor against his taste buds. His heritage had all but banished the words *too hot* from his vocabulary, but when Juan's hand hovered over a small bright orange habanero, Javy had to protest. "Seriously, Juan, it's perfect. You know what happens when you mess with perfection."

The man flashed a gap-toothed grin. "Your mama comes at me with her cast iron."

"You know it." Javy pointed at the chef as he backed toward the swinging door. "So don't touch the salsa."

"But…"

Javy bumped his way through the door and out into the dining area, shaking his head as Juan's protest followed him. Javy hoped the chef took a serious step away from the peppers, or they'd need to offer fire extinguishers as party favors.

He froze in midstride as he caught sight of what looked like an impromptu game of musical chairs taking place in front of him. The diners, who'd been seated when he walked into the kitchen moments ago, were moving out of the way, making room for the busboys and waiters, who were carrying in the tables and chairs he was pretty sure he'd left in his garage.

"What—what is this?" Javy asked. The dark stain and high-polish varnish gleamed beneath the lights.

Alex set down a table with a sigh. "Man, couldn't you've stayed in back for a few minutes longer?" his cousin complained. "We wanted to have these all set up before you saw them."

"I don't understand. How did you even know…" Javy's voice trailed off. The answer was obvious.

Emily. She'd done this for him.

"Emily told me you didn't think the varnish would be dry in time, so that's why you didn't bring the tables and chairs in before. She asked me to check on them one more time, and sure enough, they're perfect," Alex explained.

The stain and varnish had dried days ago, but Emily had given an excuse so Javy could save face with his cousin.

"Are you mad?" a hesitant voice asked.

As Emily stepped out from behind Alex, Javy could no longer deny what his heart had known all along. He loved this woman.

"No, I'm not mad. I'm…" A whirlwind of emotions twisted Javy up inside, but he couldn't possibly pull one from the restless storm. "Not mad," he finished lamely.

But Emily smiled as if he'd given her a golden compliment. "Good. I couldn't let you give up on these pieces." Walking up to him, her eyes glowing, she brushed a kiss against his cheek as she whispered, "They're too precious to waste."

"I know," Javy said.

Just like he knew this time, this opportunity with Emily was too precious to let slip by. He'd known from the start that she wasn't like the other women he'd dated—she was unique, special. He'd made a mistake with Stephanie, thinking that he could bide his time and that she'd still be waiting for him.

He wasn't going to make that mistake with Emily.

He took her hands into his, wanting to hold on and never let go. He opened his mouth to tell her how he felt, but just then his mother stepped into the dining area, stopping short just as he had when he saw the tables and chairs.

"What is this? Is this… Javy, what have you done?" Maria gasped.

Emily squeezed his hands as he met his mother's shocked

gaze. "I refinished the damaged pieces the best I could. I know they aren't an exact match—"

He didn't have the chance to give whatever explanation he might have made. Holding out a hand to stop him from talking, her eyes downcast, Maria shook her head and fled the room.

Silence fell over the restaurant, a sharp, painful contrast to the excitement and laughter only seconds before.

"Javy, I am so sorry." Regret filled Emily's gaze, dimming the excitement brimming there only seconds earlier. "This is all my fault."

"No, it isn't. What you did, having Alex bring these back here, it means a lot to me. And I'm sorry my mother isn't happy with what I've done, but the truth is what I told her. I did my best. And that's all I can do."

And he was tired of settling for second best—in his relationships and in his work at the restaurant. It was time to give life his all. Starting with the woman standing in front of him.

Emily knew little about the restaurant business, but she knew a success when she saw one, and the reopening was definitely a success. The dining area and bar were packed, and a few brave souls had even opted for outdoor seating despite the unrelenting heat.

Javy was amazing. Emily was willing to bet he talked with every patron to step through the doors, amid coordinating the staff, checking on the kitchen and taking time to introduce the band. If his mother's earlier silence had any lasting effect, Emily was unable to spot it.

They hadn't had much of a chance to talk since she'd arrived, but Emily didn't mind. It gave her a chance to watch him in action, and every now and then, their eyes would meet. Each look held a wealth of promises—promises she planned to hold him to as soon as they were done—but Emily was starting to think the closing would never happen as the band played one set after another and patrons ordered round after round. Finally, the crowd started to disperse, with nearly every customer stopping by to congratulate Javy.

"You must be exhausted," Emily murmured as he said good-night to the last of his staff.

Wrapping an arm around her shoulders, he anchored her to his side. "I'm sure I'll crash soon, but right now I'm feeling pretty invincible."

"Wow!" Emily raised her eyebrows suggestively. She reached up and gave his bicep a squeeze. "Man of steel, huh?"

Javy groaned. "Don't tempt me."

But that was exactly what Emily wanted to do—to tempt Javy beyond the restraint he'd shown the night before. "I can stay until you're done here," she offered. Even though everyone had already left, the restaurant was in nowhere near the shape it needed to be in for opening the next day. And she knew Javy would be methodical in shutting down the place before he left. Nerves jumping in her stomach, she added, "Or I could go back to my place, and you could come by when you're finished…."

Heat flared in Javy's eyes, and she waited, heart pounding, for him to say yes. The pace only picked up when he caught her hand and led the way outside to the back patio. With the starry night overhead, Emily immediately thought of the night of Kelsey and Connor's wedding. The first time she'd really talked to Javy and the first time he'd kissed her.

Had that really only been two weeks ago? It seemed too crazy that she could have fallen so far, so fast.

Don't look down, she reminded herself even as Javy pulled her into his arms in a kiss that battled with the sultry summer night with its intensity. When he finally eased away to take a much-needed breath, Emily waited for him to agree with her earlier suggestion, to go back to her place, to finish that they'd started, to…

"Marry me."

Emily blinked. The pulse still pounding in her ears was messing with her hearing. It was the only explanation. He couldn't have said…

"Marry me, Emily."

"What?"

"I love you. I want us to spend the rest of our lives together. To have kids and watch them grow…"

Even in the dim light of the patio, Emily could see the certainty and sincerity written in his dark eyes. And she absolutely wasn't imagining this—because not in a million years would she have imagined Javier Delgado proposing. But the more she listened to Javy—to his plans—the more the frantic feeling of panic threatened to crawl out from inside of her and devour her whole.

"Javy, this is crazy. My *wedding* was less than a month ago."

"It wasn't *your* wedding, Emily."

"No, of course not, but it should have been." Javy's jaw tightened, and she hurried to explain. "Not that I think I should have married Todd. That's *not* what I mean, but—"

"But what?"

"I rushed into an engagement with Todd. If I had taken more time, if I'd thought things through, I would have realized it was a mistake."

"And you think I'm a mistake." He took a step back, barriers slamming down like steel bars.

"No, I don't think that. But I never expected… I didn't think you were serious about all this. We were supposed to be having fun…." And she'd warned herself time and time again not to fall in love—for all the good it had done.

But at her words, barbed wire and electric fencing added

to the barricade already erected. "Fun?" he echoed with a harsh tone. "Funny thing about *fun* and *good times*…they always come to an end."

Her heart lurching inside her chest like a wounded animal desperate to escape, Emily ignored the "Do Not Cross" warning signs. "Please, Javy…I love you. I do," she said, her voice trembling with emotion. She'd never imagined telling him how she felt, never imagined that it would hurt *so bad.* "But…"

She'd thought she loved Todd, too. She'd closed her eyes to everything she hadn't wanted to see—Todd's silences, his secrets, his manipulation. And while she didn't want to believe Javy was *anything* like her former fiancé, she couldn't deny the way he'd initially brushed aside her questions about Stephanie, the way he still hadn't confided his plans for the restaurant to her, and now…now he was talking about the future—*their* future—as if it was written in stone and she had no say about the house with the white picket fence and about the two-point-five kids he saw living there.

"I just need time. We *both* need time. You've had a lot to deal with recently, and now tonight you're riding high on success and emotion, just like you must have been the night you and Stephanie graduated and you proposed—"

"That was *ten years* ago, Emily. You think I'm still some reckless *kid* who doesn't know better?" He gave a rough laugh. "Maybe you're right. I sure as hell don't seem to have learned my lesson."

"Javy, that's not fair. I just need some time—"

"To do what?" he demanded. "Find a better offer?"

Emily swallowed hard, no less hurt than if he'd reached out and slapped her. "No," she whispered. "Of course not."

"Then what's the problem? Either you love me enough to make a commitment or you don't." When Emily struggled to find a way to explain, Javy shook his head. His jaw hardened as he backed away from her. "Obviously you don't."

Signs of the party the night before still littered the restaurant when Javy stepped inside the next morning—straw wrappers, discarded napkins and dropped receipts. The night had been filled with laughter, excitement and anticipation but now...now he had nothing to do but clean up the mess. Too bad the debris of his relationship with Emily couldn't be swept away so easily.

He swore beneath his breath as he grabbed a broom and dustpan from the back. It sure as hell should have been. After all, she'd thrown his proposal—his heart—away like so much trash.

He was in the middle of turning sweeping into a full-contact sport when the back door opened. His heart gave an involuntary lurch when he had no reason to believe Emily would come back to him.

But the woman who stepped into the restaurant was not the one he expected, even though he probably should have.

"Mama, I didn't think you'd be here this morning."

As busy as the restaurant had been the night before and wanting to give the employees a chance to celebrate, Javy had instructed the staff to leave the cleaning for the next day. He'd thought he'd be there early enough to have everything done before the first shift. He certainly hadn't counted on his mother coming in and seeing the mess left behind.

Another mark against him—careless, irresponsible Javier—but he couldn't bring himself to care. "I'll get this cleaned up—"

"It is fine, Javier." Despite her words, he heard the tremor in her voice, saw the tears she surreptitiously tried to wipe from her cheeks.

"Mama, what's wrong?"

She shook her head. "Nothing is wrong." Running a lined hand over the tabletop, she said, "The restaurant, it has not looked so good in years. The work you have done here, all of it, your father would be so proud of."

As compliments went, Javy couldn't think of one that would mean more to Maria or to him…if he could bring himself to believe it. "You think?" he asked, the casual question unable to hide his doubt.

"Of course." Turning his face toward her, she asked, "Why do you think he wouldn't be?"

After ten years of silence, the admission didn't come easily. The words stalled in his throat, trapped by guilt and regret. Finally, though, he started talking. "We fought. Right before he got sick, the night I told you both I'd proposed to Stephanie."

Maria's eyes widened. "I told him not to talk to you when he was so angry. He needed time to calm down." They'd both needed time, but they had never had that chance.

"He said I didn't have what it took to be a good husband, that I'd never stuck with anything in my life, and when the going got tough, I was the first to get going." And when he hadn't been able to keep his promise to Stephanie, when he hadn't been able to handle the stress of running the restaurant, he'd been so sure his father was right—about everything.

"Oh, *mijo.*" Sorrow and regret filled Maria's eyes as she ran a lined hand over the back of one of the chairs. "You would think a man who could do such work would have patience but…" She shrugged. "He was a perfectionist, carving away until the piece matched the picture in his head. Maybe it works with wood, but with people, it is not so easy."

Javy recalled his father's pursuit of perfection in his work. How many times had he seen Miguel toss aside a carving he didn't think good enough? After their fight, Javy had felt like his father had done the same to him. "I know he was disappointed in me."

Maria shook her head. "We were worried. Stephanie was trouble, and you were both too young to get married and run off to chase some dream. But that was then. A long time ago, when you were just a boy. I am so sorry your papa isn't here to see you now. To see the man you've become. He would be proud of you, and he would be so ashamed of me. That is why I had to leave last night. I couldn't face what I had done."

"He would never be ashamed of you," Javy argued.

"I should have listened when you asked to change the restaurant. I should have seen you weren't my little boy anymore, but I was still seeing my *chico pequeño*. But this…" Maria waved a hand around the restaurant. "All the hard work you've done, all the time you've spent, I have no choice but to see the man you are now."

All he'd done…all the time he'd spent… Like a smack upside the head, Javy realized now where he'd gone wrong. "It's not your fault. I should have realized it would take more than words to prove I've changed."

And that was where he'd failed Emily. He'd told her all his grand plans. He hadn't even bothered to *ask* her to marry him, telling her instead about the future he already had planned, brushing aside her hard-won independence as if it meant nothing.

Was he really surprised that she saw him as no different from Todd Dunworthy or her parents, pushing her into what he wanted, into what he thought was best without asking what she wanted?

"But I still should have let you change the restaurant," Maria insisted. Lifting her chin bravely, she said, "It's not too late, *mijo*. We can still remodel, to make the place what you want it to be."

What he wanted, but not what his mother wanted…

For the first time in years, Javy could sense his father's presence beyond the shadow of their final words to each other. He could hear his boisterous voice in the echo of the laughter and music from the night before, see his strong, work-roughened hands in the carved furniture's painstaking detail, feel his love and pride in the restaurant Maria had preserved in his memory. And he understood, too, why his mother couldn't bear to change anything.

"No, Mama. That wouldn't be right, either." Taking a deep breath, he voiced the idea he'd refused to even consider for so long. The idea he'd never even had the chance to tell Emily about. "I want to look into opening a restaurant of my own. Another Delgado's, with the kind of bar and patio I've always pictured." Seeing his mother's eyes widen, he added, "It wouldn't be around here. Somewhere across town."

"Oh, Javy. It was always your papa's dream. That is why it was so hard for him to hear you wanted to leave. He knew you would need to run your own place. But me, I was selfish. I wanted you here. After Miguel died, I *needed* you here. But now it's time for you to grow up. Time to prove yourself to the girl you love."

Javy pulled back in surprise. "How did you know?"

"A mother always knows, and I did not think Emily was right for you. I thought her too much like the other girls, who made it too easy for you to walk away. But she is different."

"Yeah, she's different, all right. *She's* the one who walked away."

Reaching out, Maria pushed her index finger against his chest. "Then it is up to you."

"Up to me?" Yeah, okay, maybe he'd handled things badly with Emily, rushing forward when he should have taken things slow, but he'd poured his heart out. What more was he supposed to do?

"It's up to you," Maria repeated, "to give her a reason to come back."

Chapter Fifteen

Emily didn't know what she would have done without the fund-raiser and fashion show to keep her busy. She'd thrown herself into the event, coordinating the clothes, the alterations and the "models." She'd found supporters to donate the items for the auction, as well as backers to match what money they raised.

When she'd initially balked at the suggested asking price per person for the dinner to follow the fashion show, it had been her mother who had reassured her.

"It isn't like women my age are frequently asked to walk the runway," her mother had said wryly. "Believe me, they will pay whatever the price to make sure friends and family are in the audience, watching."

So Emily had agreed to the price, and they'd sold enough tickets to move into a larger ballroom.

Given the chance, she would likely have panicked at the

thought of so many people attending an event she'd coordinated, an event that could fall apart and be her second biggest, most public failure in a whole month. But she'd simply made sure she didn't have time to think. Not about the fund-raiser's possible failure or about the definite failure of her relationship with Javy.

Standing backstage as the women primped for the show, Emily felt a small smile tug at her lips. No use telling them this wasn't fashion week in Paris; they were giving their one shot as models all they had.

"I still can't believe you've done all this hard work, and you're not even going to have a little fun."

As Emily turned to face her cousin, her smile grew. Kelsey looked amazing in a strapless emerald-green cocktail dress. A few weeks ago she never would have worn such a revealing outfit, forget taking a stroll down a catwalk, but her love for Connor had given her an added confidence and a spark in her eyes, which left Emily quietly sighing with envy.

"Are you kidding? I worked with the design students, picking out perfect clothes for Lauren and the other women from the shelter to model. I don't think I would have enjoyed anything more."

"I know, and everyone's raving about the job you did. Not that it's any surprise. No one is ever better dressed than you are. I mean, look at you." Kelsey gestured to Emily's gown— a gold sheath with rhinestone straps and a beaded bodice that whispered down the length of her body. "So why aren't you modeling any of the clothes?"

"I'm the emcee," Emily protested, "although I still say we should have had Trey do the job. He's the pro." Kelsey's friend Trey Jamison was a DJ who frequently worked at the weddings her cousin coordinated. "I would have rather stayed backstage to help with hair and makeup and all the outfit changes we're doing. I'm perfectly happy here."

A knowing look in her brown eyes, Kelsey leaned forward to give Emily a hug. "No, you're not," she whispered. "But I hope you will be."

Any response Emily might have made was prevented by the tears in her throat.

"You're going to do an amazing job, Emily."

She'd expected the encouraging words from Kelsey, but she hadn't anticipated hearing them from her mother. Turning, she met her mother's gaze. Charlene wore an eggplant suit with a fitted jacket and a knee-length skirt. With her short brown hair and makeup perfectly styled, and wearing an amazing amethyst pendant on a pearl choker, her mother looked ready to walk the runway herself…except Charlene had never offered, and Emily hadn't asked.

Regretting the rift that still gaped between them, Emily offered a tentative smile. "Thank you, Mother. And thank you for coming."

"Kelsey, I'd like to talk to my daughter for a moment if you don't mind."

"Of course not, Aunt Charlene." With a final hug and whispered encouragement, Kelsey slipped away.

"You've done a remarkable thing here, Emily."

"Thank you. I'm really pleased—" and amazed "—with how well everything has turned out."

"You should be. After all, you did this all on your own," Charlene said, and for the first time, Emily realized her mother wasn't worried or exasperated or afraid she would fail. Instead, Charlene was hurt at being pushed aside.

"I'm sorry, Mother. I didn't mean to exclude you, but I guess I was afraid."

"Of what?"

"That you would think I was doing everything wrong and take over."

Charlene sighed, ready to brush aside the words, but Emily refused to be dismissed. "You've done it my whole life. Why couldn't you let me make my own decisions? And my own mistakes?"

"I suppose it was because *we* were afraid."

Expecting a denial, Emily didn't know what surprised her more—that her mother had answered or the answer she'd given. "Why?"

"We were afraid of losing you."

Emily shook her head. "You weren't going to lose me."

"Don't make it sound so ridiculous." Reaching out, Charlene turned Emily toward the full-length mirror. Standing over her shoulder, her mother adjusted one of the rhinestone clips holding her hair. "Sometimes you look so like your aunt Olivia, I feel like I'm seeing a ghost."

The ghost of mistakes past, Emily thought.

"Is that why you've always kept such a close eye on everything I've done? Because of Olivia?"

"She was such a beautiful girl," Charlene said with enough of a wry twist to her smile to make Emily wonder if her mother had once been jealous of her younger sister-in-law. "Your father adored her. He was the protective big brother, always looking out for her. And Olivia... Well, with the trouble she liked to get into, she needed someone willing to bail her out."

"I don't remember her. Aileen says she has a few memories of going to an amusement park and of Olivia letting her wear lipstick to her fifth birthday party."

"That's probably one of the last family events Olivia attended. Your father was devastated when she ran away. He kept hoping she would return, but years went by with no contact, and you…" Charlene rested her hands on her daughter's shoulders. "You were so like her."

"I've seen the pictures," Emily said, but her mother shook her head.

"It isn't just how you looked. It was the way you acted. The way you walked and talked. How you could sing and dance… So much of that was Olivia, yet she couldn't have had an influence on you. As you said, you were too young to remember."

"Maybe it was something in our genes."

"I think that's what your father…what both of us were afraid of. That along with Olivia's talent and beauty, you had inherited her stubborn independence, and that someday you'd leave us the same way she had. And we couldn't bear the thought. But it was a mistake. Your father and I see that now. We were trying so desperately to hold on, we were holding you back. I hope you can forgive us. We know we have to let you go. It's your time to fly."

Hearing her mother's words, Emily realized she didn't need a parachute. Not when she was finally ready to stretch her wings.

The moment Emily stepped out onstage, she knew everything was going to be okay. Better than okay. The spotlight shone down on her like the full moon had the night of the wedding. And she felt just like she had when Javy pulled her onto the dance floor. His confidence had encouraged her every step of the way, and she refused to believe it was too late for the two of them.

She no longer needed the time she'd asked for. She was done second-guessing herself. Yes, she'd made a mistake with Todd, but the bigger mistake would be in failing to recognize that *Javy* was not Todd.

Just like her parents had built a world around her similarities to her aunt Olivia, Emily, too, had gotten stuck in a rut of comparisons—thinking she had to protect herself so Javy couldn't hurt her the way Todd had, focusing on Javy's previous relationship so she wouldn't be surprised if Javy cheated on her, like Todd had, refusing to move forward with Javy in case all her hopes and dreams came crashing down, like her hopes and dreams with Todd had.

But the one difference she'd overlooked was the most important—Javy loved her in a way Todd never had.

Hope shining brighter than the spotlight, Emily stepped up to the microphone and started the welcome speech she'd written. "Good evening, ladies and gentlemen, and welcome to the first annual Second Chance Fashion Show."

As she introduced the models and described their outfits, she took a moment to enjoy watching the women on the catwalk as much as the appreciative audience. Kelsey strutted her stuff with a flirtatious smile, although Emily noticed her cousin's gaze never left Connor, who sat at a front-row table. And Lauren, who had inspired the whole fund-raiser, practically floated down the runway, looking amazing in an ivory gown that had once belonged to Emily but had been expertly tailored to fit Lauren's smaller frame.

Seeing the other woman's new confidence made the entire evening a success regardless of how much money the fundraiser earned.

"How about a round of applause for our wonderful models?" Emily called out as the last woman left the stage. She waited until the applause died down before adding, "The best part of our fashion show is that the clothes worn tonight will be donated to the Second Chance shelter." Another round of applause echoed through the ballroom. "But the evening isn't over yet. We have our auction items, guaranteed to send the bidding through the roof."

More applause followed, and Emily went on to announce

the first item up for auction—a weekend trip to the red rocks of Sedona. She went through item after item, recognizing that her parents and their friends were pushing up the bids in an effort to outdo each other. She didn't care; their efforts raised money for the charity, and she sensed how much her father was enjoying himself with every bid he made.

Only one time did Emily falter. Even though she knew the item was part of the auction, she still stumbled when she came across the romantic dinner for two—at Delgado's Restaurant.

Ignoring the notes on the cards in front of her, Emily gazed out at the audience. Most of the people in attendance had been at the wedding only weeks ago, the very people whose opinions had mattered to her so much, she'd been afraid to dance with Javy, too concerned with what they might think…until he'd taken her in his arms, and from that moment on, she hadn't cared about anyone but him.

"This next item may not be the most extravagant on tonight's list, but it's one that means the most to me. The restaurant belongs to Javier Delgado, and without him, this entire night wouldn't have taken place. He gave me the confidence to believe I can do anything I put my mind to and to trust in myself and my own decisions. I let him down when I forgot that recently, and I hope I'll have the chance to make it up to him." Taking a deep breath to reclaim her composure, Emily said, "Now, let's start the bidding."

As she had throughout the evening, Emily started the bidding low, giving the audience the chance to raise the stakes offer by offer. An unexpected feeling of pride welled up inside her, bringing an unsuppressed smile to her face, as the amount continued to climb. She only wished Javy was there to see it. When a brief silence fell after the last bid, Emily scanned the audience. "Going once, going twice—"

"Ten thousand dollars," a familiar masculine voice called out.

Excited murmurs broke out in the audience, but to Emily, the words meant nothing. She was too shocked to see Javy cutting through the tables to register what he'd said. Her gaze soaked up the sight of him like the desert in a rainstorm until all the emotions welling up inside her threatened to overflow. He looked gorgeous in black slacks and a dove-grey silk shirt, the love shining in his eyes making it impossible for Emily to look away. Her heart pounded as he drew closer, but he didn't stop at the edge of the stage. He hopped up, his long, confident strides closing the distance until the flimsy podium was the only barrier between them.

Emily would have gladly pushed it out of the way, but she wasn't sure she could stand on her own. Her hands gripped the wood tightly enough to leave dents, and even though she'd talked almost nonstop the whole evening, she couldn't think of a single thing to say.

Good thing Javy seemed to have his own speech prepared. "There is one condition," he said, his dark eyes never leaving Emily's. "You have to agree to have dinner with me."

"Dinner?" Emily echoed.

"Well, yeah." His grin held a touch of vulnerability, which went straight to her heart. "Not much of a romantic dinner if I'm eating by myself."

"But…you donated dinner at the restaurant. You don't have to bid on it."

"It's for a good cause, and I won't rob anyone else of the chance to try our food. I'll donate another dinner for the auction, one that can be redeemed at our current location now or at our second location, which will be opening by the end of the year."

Emily was vaguely aware of more applause from the audience and realized Javy was close enough to the microphone that the crowd could hear their conversation, but she honestly didn't care. "You're opening a second restaurant?"

"With a huge sports bar area and a patio, just the way I've always pictured—"

"And your mother gets to keep her restaurant exactly the way your father made it."

Javy nodded. "We both get what we want...just the way it should be."

Emily read the promise in his expression, one that had nothing to do with his mother or the restaurant and everything to do with *them*.

"Besides," he said, glancing over his shoulder at their audience, "if I'm willing to pay ten thousand dollars for dinner at my own place, you know the food's gotta be good. But it's the company that will be worth every penny if Emily will agree to have dinner with me."

"Ten thousand..." she whispered, her voice trailing off in disbelief. "You can't—"

"I want to, believe me. I've been trying to repay that money for years. Connor won't take it, and neither will your dad," he said wryly. "This was the best thing I could think of to do with it. But there's still my condition."

"To have dinner with you?"

"Just dinner," he emphasized. "I love you, Emily. I was afraid if I waited too long, you'd slip away and I'd lose you. But I held on too hard. I moved too fast, trying to push you into what I wanted when really all I want is to be with you. So what do you say?"

"I say yes." To dinner and everything he'd already asked for—marriage, family, forever... "I love you, too. And I'm sorry I made you doubt that, especially after everything you did to prove the kind of man you are—the kind of man your father would be so proud of. It was never you I didn't trust, but myself. It was safer to believe what we had wasn't serious than to admit how quickly I'd fallen for you."

"Yeah, well, turns out I was wrong about that."

Emily frowned. "About what?"

"The good times haven't come to an end," he promised, his dark eyes intent on hers. "In fact, they're just beginning. So what do you say we get out of here?"

Gradually becoming aware once again of the fund-raiser and the dozens of people watching, even though Javy had already guided her away from the podium and the live microphone, Emily protested reluctantly. "Javy, I can't. We're in the middle of the auction and—"

"Hey, everyone," a male voice announced, and she turned to see Trey Jamison adjusting the mic. "I'm here to finish auctioning off tonight's items, but how about a big hand for Emily Wilson, who made this whole night possible."

Her cousin's friend flashed her a wink before he picked up her notes and got to work like the professional he was.

Realization hitting a bit too late, Emily slanted Javy a glance as he led her to the side of the stage and the ballroom exit. "You planned this, didn't you? For Trey to take over with the auction? And let me guess, Kelsey was in on it, too."

"Guilty as charged," he admitted without looking the least bit repentant. "But it was strictly for your own good."

"Oh, and you think you know what's best for me," Emily challenged.

"I do." Pulling her into his arms, he vowed, "I am."

And how could she argue with that?

Epilogue

"How angry do you think your parents are going to be?" Javy asked.

Turning away from the view of the Las Vegas Strip, Emily smiled at her husband of fifteen minutes. "Are you kidding? Kelsey's the one I'll really have to look out for. I'm sure she would have loved to coordinate a wedding for me where I was actually the one to get married. What about your mother? Are you going to be dodging skillets when we get back?"

"Mama's going to be so glad I'm married, I think she'll forgive me. Of course, she'll want to have a huge party once we get back."

"My family will, too."

"I say we have one big reception at Dos Delgado and invite everyone, since we're all family now."

"That sounds perfect."

Although Emily doubted the party at Javy's new restaurant

would be what her parents had in mind, they'd surprised her the past few months by being far more accepting than she'd ever believed possible. Especially once she made it clear how much she loved Javy and how happy he made her.

"And what about you?" Javy asked as he crossed the honeymoon suite.

Even though they'd decided to forgo the full-on wedding ceremony, they had both dressed for the occasion—Emily in a simple white sheath with a touch of beading along the V-neckline and Javy in a dark gray suit. He'd already tossed aside his tie, removed his jacket and rolled up the sleeves of his light gray shirt, revealing a casual style that suited him and never failed to steal Emily's breath. Too focused on how sexy her new husband was, she missed the point of his question.

"What about me?" A pop of a cork punctuated her question as he opened the bottle of champagne that had been waiting for them in the honeymoon suite.

"How disappointed are you not to have a huge wedding?"

"Not at all. Our wedding was exactly what I wanted." She'd been a little concerned they might end up at some drive-through chapel of love, but the place Javy found had been perfect—a small church filled with candles and flowers and just the two of them.

"Are you sure?" He handed her a glass, his gaze intent on hers. "I was at your would-be wedding, remember? Just a few months ago, *that* was exactly what you wanted."

"Yes, it was," Emily agreed, thinking how wrong—and how lucky—she had been. "I needed the designer gown, the nursery's worth of flowers, the orchestra and silly ice sculptures to make up for the one thing that wedding didn't have—a groom I loved and one who loved me."

Setting aside their glasses before she had a chance to do little more than taste the sparkling bubbles against her tongue, Javy pulled Emily into his arms. "You have that now," he vowed.

Joy and love and happiness spinning inside her, Emily couldn't agree more. In Javy, she had everything she'd ever wanted—a man who loved her for herself, who believed in her, who had been willing to wait to make love, because once upon a time that was how she had imagined her perfect wedding night.

He could have seduced her into his bed weeks ago, and Emily would have been more than willing to be there. He hadn't, though, and she loved him even more for it. But now, finally, the wait was over.

Any nerves Emily might have had melted away beneath Javy's kiss. He made her feel desired and cherished. Each fiercely tender touch let her know that this was as much about her heart as it was about her body, and that he felt the same.

As her wedding gown slid to the floor, his lips drifted over her skin like liquid gold, leaving her breathless, boneless, trembling in their wake. Just when she feared her legs could no longer support her, Javy scooped her into his arms and placed her in the middle of the bed. Her head spun at the sudden movement, and she had no hope of regaining any sense of balance as he followed her down.

The welcomed weight and heat of his body pressed her into the soft mattress, and she instantly sought out the buttons on his shirt. Her startled gaze flew to his when he closed his hand over hers, stilling her movements. His expression was intense, serious, but not enough to hide the spark in his dark eyes. "You should know," he said, his voice a rough whisper, "I've never done this before." At the bemused lift of Emily's eyebrows, he added, "Made love to a married woman."

Fighting a smile, she asked, "Do you think it will make a difference?"

Lowering his head to brush his lips against hers, he declared, "All the difference in the world."

Emily felt the difference in his kiss, in his touch. Desire poured through her veins as he brushed aside her bra and panties. The rough whisper of breath against her skin became a heated promise his lips and tongue kept as he teased her throat, her breasts, her belly....

He stopped only long enough to strip away his clothes before he was kissing her again, his weight braced on his elbows. Emily ran her hands across his shoulders and back, loving the play of lean muscle beneath his smooth, tanned skin. He groaned when she reached the small of his back and pulled him tighter to her.

He broke the kiss and pulled back to meet her gaze as he vowed, "I love you."

The words always sent a warm rush of amazement straight to her heart, and every time, Emily saw that same feeling of awe mirrored in Javy's dark eyes. But she didn't need words to echo his response. Instead, her body arched to meet his in an instant so perfect, so...*right*.

She cried out his name as he moved inside her, the rush of emotion bringing tears to her eyes. The beauty of the moment built and grew until waves of pleasure broke over her, stealing her breath as they pulled her under, and then seeming to gently carry her back to shore—to safety, to the warmth and comfort of Javy's arms.

Moments later, as she drifted off to sleep, resting her hand against Javy's chest, Emily felt the steady beat of his heart and the still new weight of the ring on her finger. Her wedding night was more than she could have dreamed—a night of many firsts filled with a love destined to last.

* * * * *

Harlequin offers a romance for every mood!
See below for a sneak peek from our
paranormal romance line, Silhouette® Nocturne™.
Enjoy a preview of REUNION by USA TODAY *bestselling*
author Lindsay McKenna.

Aella closed her eyes and sensed a distinct shift, like movement from the world around her to the unseen world.

She opened her eyes. And had a slight shock at the man standing ten feet away. He wasn't just any man. Her heart leaped and pounded. He reminded her of a fierce warrior from an ancient civilization. Incan? She wasn't sure but she felt his deep power and masculinity.

I'm Aella. Are you the guardian of this sacred site? she asked, hoping her telepathy was strong.

Fox's entire body soared with joy. Fox struggled to put his personal pleasure aside.

Greetings, Aella. I'm the assistant guardian to this sacred area. You may call me Fox. How can I be of service to you, Aella? he asked.

I'm searching for a green sphere. A legend says that the Emperor Pachacuti had seven emerald spheres created for the Emerald Key necklace. He had seven of his priestesses and priests travel the world to hide these spheres from evil forces. It is said that when all seven spheres are found, restrung and worn, that Light will return to the Earth. The fourth sphere is here, at your sacred site. Are you aware of it? Aella held her breath. She loved looking at him, especially his sensual mouth. The desire to kiss him came out of nowhere.

Fox was stunned by the request. *I know of the Emerald Key*

necklace because I served the emperor at the time it was created. However, I did not realize that one of the spheres is here.

Aella felt sad. Why? Every time she looked at Fox, her heart felt as if it would tear out of her chest. *May I stay in touch with you as I work with this site?* she asked.

Of course. Fox wanted nothing more than to be here with her. To absorb her ephemeral beauty and hear her speak once more.

Aella's spirit lifted. What *was* this strange connection between them? Her curiosity was strong, but she had more pressing matters. In the next few days, Aella knew her life would change forever. How, she had no idea….

Look for REUNION
by USA TODAY bestselling author Lindsay McKenna,
available April 2010, only from Silhouette® Nocturne™.

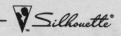

SPECIAL EDITION

INTRODUCING A BRAND-NEW MINISERIES
FROM *USA TODAY* BESTSELLING AUTHOR

KASEY MICHAELS

SECOND-CHANCE BRIDAL

At twenty-eight, widowed single mother
Elizabeth Carstairs thinks she's left love behind
forever....until she meets Will Hollingsbrook.
Her sons' new baseball coach is the handsomest
man she's ever seen—and the more time they
spend together, the more undeniable the
connection between them. But can Elizabeth
leave the past behind and open her heart to
a second chance at love?

FIND OUT IN

SUDDENLY A BRIDE

*Available in April
wherever books are sold.*

Visit Silhouette Books at www.eHarlequin.com

SSE65517

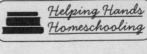

HARLEQUIN® *Romance*®

ROMANCE, RIVALRY AND A FAMILY REUNITED

THE BRIDES *of* BELLA ROSA

William Valentine and his beloved wife, Lucia, live
a beautiful life together, but when his former love Rosa
and the secret family they had together resurface,
an instant rivalry is formed. Can these families
get through the past and come together as one?

*Step into the world of Bella Rosa
beginning this April with*

Beauty and the Reclusive Prince
by

RAYE MORGAN

Eight volumes to collect and treasure!

www.eHarlequin.com

HRI7650

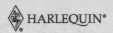

HARLEQUIN *Presents*

2 Stories in 1

HER MEDITERRANEAN PLAYBOY

Sexy and dangerous—he wants you in his bed!

The sky is blue, the azure sea is crashing against the golden sand and the sun is hot.

The conditions are perfect for a scorching Mediterranean seduction from two irresistible untamed playboys!

Indulge your senses with these two delicious stories

A MISTRESS AT THE ITALIAN'S COMMAND
by *Melanie Milburne*

ITALIAN BOSS, HOUSEKEEPER MISTRESS
by *Kate Hewitt*

Available April 2010 from Harlequin Presents!

www.eHarlequin.com

HP12910

REQUEST YOUR FREE BOOKS!
2 FREE NOVELS PLUS 2 FREE GIFTS!

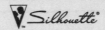

SPECIAL EDITION
Life, Love and Family!

YES! Please send me 2 FREE Silhouette® Special Edition® novels and my 2 FREE gifts (gifts are worth about $10). After receiving them, if I don't wish to receive any more books, I can return the shipping statement marked "cancel." If I don't cancel, I will receive 6 brand-new novels every month and be billed just $4.24 per book in the U.S. or $4.99 per book in Canada. That's a saving of 15% off the cover price! It's quite a bargain! Shipping and handling is just 50¢ per book in the U.S. and 75¢ per book in Canada.* I understand that accepting the 2 free books and gifts places me under no obligation to buy anything. I can always return a shipment and cancel at any time. Even if I never buy another book from Silhouette, the two free books and gifts are mine to keep forever.

235 SDN E4NC 335 SDN E4NN

Name	(PLEASE PRINT)

Address	Apt. #

City	State/Prov.	Zip/Postal Code

Signature (if under 18, a parent or guardian must sign)

Mail to the Silhouette Reader Service:
IN U.S.A.: P.O. Box 1867, Buffalo, NY 14240-1867
IN CANADA: P.O. Box 609, Fort Erie, Ontario L2A 5X3

Not valid for current subscribers to Silhouette Special Edition books.

Want to try two free books from another line?
Call 1-800-873-8635 or visit www.morefreebooks.com.

* Terms and prices subject to change without notice. Prices do not include applicable taxes. N.Y. residents add applicable sales tax. Canadian residents will be charged applicable provincial taxes and GST. Offer not valid in Quebec. This offer is limited to one order per household. All orders subject to approval. Credit or debit balances in a customer's account(s) may be offset by any other outstanding balance owed by or to the customer. Please allow 4 to 6 weeks for delivery. Offer available while quantities last.

Your Privacy: Silhouette is committed to protecting your privacy. Our Privacy Policy is available online at www.eHarlequin.com or upon request from the Reader Service. From time to time we make our lists of customers available to reputable third parties who may have a product or service of interest to you. If you would prefer we not share your name and address, please check here. ☐

Help us get it right—We strive for accurate, respectful and relevant communications. To clarify or modify your communication preferences, visit us at www.ReaderService.com/consumerschoice.